• • • • • •

"It don't matter," Cicely said between puffs. "I just wanna have fun tonight. If she comes, I'll get her. If not, I'm still getting turnt!"

"You got some of these?" Toya asked. She produced more goodies from her purse. This time it was a 3-pack box of condoms.

"No," Cicely said. Her eyes were dazzling. "You think I should stop and get some?"

"You can have one of mine, if you need it," Toya said. "You think you might need the other one?" she asked Sandra. "Derrick and Chris are supposed to come."

Sandra smiled and blushed.

"No, I think she might need hers for *Peter*," Cicely said with a laugh.

"Peter? Peter *Scott*?" Toya asked.

"Yeah, that's her new boo-thang," Cicely informed her.

"No, it's not," Sandra countered.

"Uh-oh! I didn't know about that!" Toya squawked. "You definitely need to get you some of this," she said, passing the bottle of *mostly Kool-Aid* to the front. "That way you won't chicken out again. Pass the blunt!" she told Cicely.

Cicely reluctantly gave her the blunt as Sandra took the bottle. She gazed upon the concoction's soft, red tint. She removed the cap and brought the top to her nose and took a whiff. It smelled strong. And sweet. She looked over at Cicely, wondering if she would offer any opposition.

But Cicely said, "It's our last senior party. *Forever*. Might as well turn up!"

"Yeah, might as well!" Toya agreed. "Go on, girl! *Peer pressure!*"

Cicely laughed. Sandra did too. She couldn't believe she actually said the words *peer pressure*. That made the whole idea of drinking and smoking even more taboo. Undeniably so.

• • • • • •

1

FAST GIRLS AT FINLEY HIGH

FAST GIRLS

GIRLS

AT FINLEY HIGH

KEITH THOMAS WALKER

KEITHWALKERBOOKS, INC
This is a UMS production

FAST GIRLS AT FINLEY HIGH

KEITHWALKERBOOKS

Publishing Company
KeithWalkerBooks, Inc.
P.O. Box 331585
Fort Worth, TX 76163

For information write
KeithWalkerBooks, Inc.
P.O. Box 331585
Fort Worth, TX 76163

All characters in this book have no existence outside the
imagination of the author and have no relation whatsoever to
anyone bearing the same name or names. They are not even
distantly inspired by any individual known or unknown to the
author and all incidents are pure invention.

ISBN-13 DIGIT: 978-0-9882180-8-6
ISBN-10 DIGIT: 0988218089
Library of Congress Control Number: 2015906304
Manufactured in the United States of America

First Edition

Visit us at www.keithwalkerbooks.com

This book is for Jasmine

Congratulations to Jasmine Walker whose poems *I Don't Know What Love is and Peer Pressure* are proudly featured in this novel. You go girl!

MORE BOOKS BY
KEITH THOMAS WALKER

Fixin' Tyrone
How to Kill Your Husband
A Good Dude
Riding the Corporate Ladder
The Finley Sisters' Oath of Romance
Blow by Blow
Jewell and the Dapper Dan
Harlot
Plan C (And More KWB Shorts)
Dripping Chocolate
The Realest Ever
Jackson Memorial
Sleeping With the Strangler
Life After
Blood for Isaiah
Brick House
Brick House 2

NOVELLAS

Might be Bi (Part One)
Harder

POETRY COLLECTION

Poor Righteous Poet

FINLEY HIGH SERIES

Prom Night at Finley High
Fast Girls at Finley High

Visit keithwalkerbooks.com for information about these and upcoming titles from KeithWalkerBooks

ACKNOWLEGMENTS

Of course I would like to thank God, first and foremost, for giving me the creativity and drive to pursue my dreams and the understanding that I am nothing without Him. I would like to thank my wife for being my first and most important critic, and I would like to thank my mother for always pushing me to be the best I can be. I would like to thank Janae Hampton for being the best advisor, supporter and little sister a brother could ever have. I would also like to thank (in no particular order) Beulah Neveu, Deloris Harper, Denise Fizer, Shelee Stevenson, Melissa Carter, Cathy Atchison, Lanita Irvin, Ramona Weathersbee, Jason Owens, Sharon Blount, BRAB Book Club, and Uncle Steven Thomas, one love. I'd like to thank everyone who purchased and enjoyed one of my books. Everything I do has always been to please you. I know there are folks who mean the world to me that I'm failing to mention. I apologize ahead of time. Rest assured I'm grateful for everything you've done for me!

FAST GIRLS AT FINLEY HIGH

CHAPTER ONE
SCHOOL FLOW

I wish I had a big front yard
With bright green grass stretching out far
I'd stand there and gaze the stars
I bet I could see clear to Mars
I'd mow and trim it crisp and neat
And water from 2 a.m. till 3
Stretch a hammock between two trees
And sway with the wind, sipping tea
But Mom tells me, "Girl, life is hard
Without Dad here to do his part"
These project grounds are dry and hard
I wish I had a big front yard

-KTW

    Toya rolled over and squinted at the bright sunshine peeking through her bedroom curtains. She cursed the sun's punctuality before rolling back onto her side. She returned her attention to her cellphone, waiting for *Big Daddy* to respond to her last message.

Derrick, whose government name was certainly not "Big Daddy," gave himself the nickname after scrolling through Toya's call log one day. It took nearly five minutes to get her phone back after he decided to play *jealous boyfriend* that afternoon. His invasion into her privacy brought him to the conclusion that Toya had way too many boys' names and numbers in her phone.

"Who is all these dudes?" he'd asked. "You don't need all these fools in your phone."

"You not my man," Toya had told him. "If you ain't my man, you can't tell me how many boys I can have in my phone."

Toya thought she had made it clear with her tone (and the flirtatious way she smiled at him) that Derrick could and *should* be her man, at which point he'd have the authority to ask her to remove the offensive numbers from her phone.

But either Derrick didn't pick up on the not-so-subtle hints or he wasn't interested in being her man officially, because he had an alternate suggestion:

"You need to change my name to '*Big Daddy*,' so I'll be different from all them other clowns. When you with them, I want them to see 'Big Daddy' come up on your phone when I call."

That wasn't the pledge of commitment Toya was hoping for. In fact, it was the exact opposite. It sounded like Derrick was acknowledging that they weren't in an exclusive relationship, and that was fine with him. But it also sounded like he was a little jealous of the other boys in Toya's life – and that was something that made her happy. So she changed his name to "Big Daddy" in her phone. It always brought a smile to her face when she saw it.

What you wearing 2day? he texted.

I dont know, she typed back.

Some leggins? he asked a few seconds later.

I dont know, she said again.

You should wear some leggins, he suggested.

Toya grinned. Her whole body grew warmer by a couple of degrees. She knew why he wanted her to wear leggings, but she wanted him to say it.

Why?

She sat up in bed while she waited for his response. The alarm clock on her dresser indicated it was 7:17 am. She had to leave the house at eight to make it to Finley High by the time the first bell rang at 8:25. Her mom woke her up seventeen minutes ago. Toya had done nothing since then but check for messages and comments on all of her social websites and apps. Sometimes she felt like she needed an assistant to keep up with everything.

"Can I wear this?"

Toya looked up and registered annoyance at the sight of her little sister Kim. The girl had a pair of Toya's jeans in hand.

"No!" she snapped, mostly out of reflex. "Where'd you get my pants?"

"They were in the dirty clothes."

"*Ewww.* You nasty. Why you wanna wear dirty jeans to school."

"'Cause I know you won't let me wear any clean ones."

Toya had to acknowledge that her sister's reasoning was sound. The girls were roughly the same size. Toya considered herself *fine* and often told Kim she was chunky. But just because they could wear the same clothes didn't mean they should. Toya thought her little sister had hygiene issues, which were evident by her willingness to wear dirty pants today.

"You gon' get them even more dirty," she complained.

"How?" Kim wondered.

She was a tall girl with grown woman-sized boobs and thick thighs, like her big sister. Toya was curvy in the eighth grade too, but she didn't think she had it going on like Kim did. Because of her banging body, Toya doubted if her little sister would make it out of high school before she had her first baby. And she was forever grateful that she was five years older. She would graduate this year, but Kim wouldn't make it to Finley High until next year. Toya knew God was looking out for her, because she would've gone crazy by now if she had her dumb little sister following her around school. That would've been the worst thing *ever*.

"You always carrying pens in your pockets," Toya told her.

"No, I don't."

"And you don't pay attention when you sit down," Toya continued, her eyebrows bunched together. "You'll sit in throw-up or *whatever*. You don't give a damn."

"No I won't, Toya. I swear I'll bring them back clean."

"How you gon' bring back some *dirty* jeans *clean*? That don't even make sense."

"*Pleeeease?*"

"Fine. Whatever. Get out my room!" Toya snarled.

Kim took the tongue-lashing like a champ. She smiled broadly and even said, "Thank you!" before taking off.

Toya rolled her eyes, and then her mood brightened when her phone vibrated in her hand. She saw that Derrick had responded to her last question.

Yo booty swole, he said, in response to why she should wear leggings.

Toya agreed that it was, and she appreciated Derrick for noticing. But she typed, Is that all you think about?

Rather than answer that, he asked, You coming to my house 4 lunch today?

Toya grinned as she typed, Maybe

She plugged the charger into her cellphone and left it on the bed while she hurried to the bathroom to bathe and get ready for school. Thirty minutes later she was fully dressed in a tight tee-shirt that had the word "*Boom!*" scrawled across her ample bosoms along with the black leggings Derrick requested.

As she turned to the side, checking out her physique in the mirror, she couldn't help but agree with plans Finley High had to adjust their dress code next year. The principal wanted to outlaw tights, leggings and yoga pants unless the student's shirt or sweater was long enough to fully cover their butt. Mr. Walters went as far as naming the new initiative the "No Butts Rule."

He might as well have called it the "*Toya Rule*," because she had to be exactly who he was thinking about when he decided they needed to make a change. Her derriere was beautifully round and plump. The stretch pants left little to the imagination. Coupled with the tight tee, she might as well have been wearing a cat suit to school.

Toya chuckled at her sinful deliciousness and went back to her bed to retrieve her phone. It took nearly twenty shots to get the perfect selfie; with most of her face not in the frame, because she hadn't put on her makeup yet. But she had plenty of patience when it came to taking selfies.

She posted the picture on Facebook with the caption "#SchoolFlow" beneath it. She made sure to turn her hips in the pic, because Derrick wasn't the only follower she had who appreciated her bubble butt.

She sat her phone next to the sink and watched it buzz with multiple notifications while she styled her hair and put on makeup. When she was done, about ten minutes had passed, and she had 18 "Likes" on her picture and four comments:

"Damn!"

"I see ya"

"Girl, you need to quit" Of course that comment was from a female hater.

And someone asked her, "You go to OCC?" referring to Overbrook Meadows Community College.

Toya wasn't concerned that she didn't know the man who asked that question. Just because he was her Facebook "friend" didn't mean she had ever met him in real life. She also wasn't concerned that the guy appeared to be in his late twenties. Toya was actually flattered that some people assumed she had graduated from high school already.

Technically, since she was 19, she knew that she should be a freshman in college. But she flunked a grade, and as it was she had two weeks to go before she graduated from Finley High School.

She clicked the "Like" button on the stranger's OCC comment.

She then noticed that she had a new follower on Instagram. Considering that she didn't post this morning's pic on Instagram, she was definitely feeling herself at that point.

She headed to the kitchen to see what Mama had on the stove. It smelled like bacon. Her mother warned that greasy foods would go straight to her thighs, but Toya considered that a life goal, rather than an admonition. She was grateful for any meal that made her thighs grow thicker. The juicier they got the better.

• • • • • •

When she got to the kitchen, Toya found her mother putting the finishing touches on the family's breakfast. This morning Pamela made bacon and eggs and buttery biscuits. Toya's mother was an attractive woman with smooth, dark skin and youthful features. Toya noticed that for someone who complained about what her kids ate so often, she sure did feed them a lot of food that was overflowing with cholesterol.

Toya took a seat across from her little brother Ricky at the kitchen table and grinned as he shoveled a spoonful of scrambled eggs in his mouth. Ricky was a cutie. He had big, curious eyes and a head full of hair that would look awesome when he got it braided or plaited down on his skull.

Pamela approached and deposited a plate in front of her oldest daughter. Toya's mouth began to water as she reached for her fork. But her mother didn't back away from the table. Toya looked up at her with a guarded expression.

"Umm, thank you," she said.

"Yeah, whatever," her mother quipped. Her hands were on her hips now.

"What's wrong with you?" Toya mumbled as she folded a slice of bacon in her mouth.

"Why don't you tell me where you been going after lunch?" her mother said.

Toya sighed roughly through her nostrils. "Mama, we already talked about this."

"I know. And I know you been lying."

"I haven't been lying."

"Then tell me your story again," Pamela dared her. "And I already talked to Mr. Sproles. He said he's not counting you absent because you're late to his class after lunch. He said you're not coming at all."

Toya was momentarily stunned by that. She hadn't expected her mother to do so much research this late in the game.

"Mama, I do go to his class. But they don't give us enough time after lunch, and sometimes I be real late. He takes roll before I get there."

"Toya, that's the lie you told me last week. You gon' have to do better than that."

"It's not a lie, Mama."

"Girl, do you think that man is crazy? You don't think he notices when somebody walks in his class late? He said even if he counts you absent at first, he'll correct it if you show up later."

"I bet he didn't tell you his class be so wild, he don't know who comes in there half the time," Toya said. "It be people in there who don't even take his class."

"Really, Toya? That's the story you're sticking with?"

"It's the truth, Mama. I do be going to his class."

"Do I have to follow you to school, so I can have lunch with you?" Pamela threatened.

Toya didn't respond to that. She knew her mother wouldn't do it. Technically Pamela did have the time on her hands, because her shift in the cafeteria at Jackson Memorial didn't start until two p.m. But Ricky wasn't in school yet, so her mother would have to bring him with her if she wanted to follow through with her lunch date. Ricky wasn't a terrible kid, but he was known to show out whenever he got around a crowd.

"It's only two weeks left in school," Toya reminded her. She shoved more food in her face, so she could get breakfast over with as soon as possible.

"And you think none of this matters anymore, since you about to graduate?" Pamela guessed.

Actually, those were Toya's sentiments exactly. As long as she passed Mr. Sproles class, what was the worst he could do to her in the last two weeks of school? He already told the students what their grades were last week. Toya was sitting pretty with a 79. According to Mr. Sproles' calculations, she'd have to make less than a fifty on the final exam to fail his class for the six-weeks. And even if she did fail for the six-weeks, it wouldn't be enough to fail her for the semester.

Toya knew that her credit for health class was as good as printed on her transcript already. She thought her teachers were stupid for telling the students exactly what grades they needed to pass. Rather than try harder, the information tended to make underachievers relax and try less.

"Mama, if I was skipping school, don't you think more teachers would be complaining about it?"

Pamela did think that, and she checked with the rest of Toya's instructors to see if there was a pattern. There were a few tardies reported here and there, but so far Mr. Sproles was the only teacher who registered a significant number of absences.

"Hey, baby."

Rick Sr. entered the kitchen and provided a welcome distraction. Toya continued to inhale her breakfast while her mother turned and gave her boyfriend a hug and a kiss. Rick wore Dickey pants with a long-sleeved button-down; the uniform required for his job at TC's Automotive.

Unlike most of the families in her housing project, Toya was fortunate to have two working adults in her home. The combined income provided them a decent lifestyle. Her mother and Rick both had their own car, and Toya and her sister had plenty of designer clothes. They never got clowned for wearing Payless sneakers to school.

But if she had her say, Toya thought her mom should give Rick his walking papers. He met Pamela five years ago and quickly knocked her up with Ricky. He did the *honorable* thing by shacking up with her, rather than leave her to raise their child alone. But Rick didn't propose to Pamela, and they still had no plans to get married. Aside from that, Toya heard rumors in the projects that Rick had another girlfriend nearby, and he was still sleeping with one of his other two baby-mamas.

If that wasn't bad enough, Toya and her sister Kim thought Rick gave them bad vibes sometimes. He never made a move, but Toya would swear that she caught him staring at her body in a *not-so-step-fatherly-way* a few times. She felt like Rick was too smart to initiate an encounter, but if she made the first move, she was pretty sure he wouldn't push her away.

But since nothing had happened, Toya and her sister kept their mouths closed and didn't report any of this to their mother. It was obvious Pamela loved Rick dearly. If the girls were wrong about him, their accusations might interfere with a strong and financially beneficial relationship.

Toya stuffed the last of her meal into her mouth and rose from the table before her mother could resume her lecture. She almost made it out of the kitchen before Pamela found something new to complain about.

"*Whoa*! Girl, what are you wearing?"

Toya stopped in the hallway and turned slowly. The annoyed look on her face would've been more poignant if her cheeks weren't stuffed with food.

"What I do now?" she mumbled around half a biscuit.

"I know they not letting y'all dress like that at school," Pamela ventured.

"Yes we can," Toya snapped. "The only thing we can't wear is tank tops and short skirts."

"Look at her," Pamela told her boyfriend. "Look what these kids are doing these days."

Yeah, that's just perfect, Toya thought as Rick took advantage of the opportunity to fully devour her with his eyes.

He was a tall man with cinnamon brown skin and a perfectly trimmed moustache and goatee. His hair was short with perfect lines. He wore do-rags while he slept to maintain the curvy texture on top.

"I been wearing the same thing to school all year," Toya told her mother. "Why are you waiting till now to start complaining about stuff?"

"You need to watch your mouth," Pamela told her. "You're not grown, Toya. If you think you are, feel free to get a job and move your fast tail up outta here."

"I'll be gone as soon as I can," Toya mumbled.

19

"Excuse me?"

"I said can I go to school now?"

"*Gone!*" Pamela said. "And you better not skip 4th period again today. You don't want me to come up there!"

Toya turned without another word and stormed down the hallway. Her little sister had to duck back into her room for a moment to avoid getting trampled. Toya looked furious, but she wasn't upset. Not really. This was all a show, just as her mother's lecture didn't amount to a hill of beans – nothing but a bunch of hot air.

It was Pamela's job to complain about stuff, and it was Toya's job to get indignant as she defended herself. This mama/daughter drama had been going on since grade school. But it was almost over, and that was something to be happy about. Toya had a smile on her face by the time she stepped out of their apartment and felt the warm, morning sun on her pretty brown skin.

She made it a few feet down the sidewalk before she realized she left her backpack in her room. There was nothing in it she needed today, but she went back inside to retrieve it anyway, because it was cute, and it matched the sneakers she was wearing.

CHAPTER TWO
CREEPER

When she got outside, Toya headed for her friend's apartment, but she saw Serena and her brood walking down the sidewalk already.

"Hey, wait up!" Toya called.

Her homegirl looked back and stopped to wait on her.

Serena and Toya were not as close as they once were. Their relationship became even more strained after the huge incident on prom night last Saturday. Serena blamed Toya for spilling the beans about her pregnancy. But Toya felt the embarrassment Serena endured was ultimately her own fault, because she was the one who got pregnant.

"Hey," she said when Toya caught up with them. "You walking today?"

"Might as well," Toya said, and the group got moving again.

Before they headed to Finley High, Serena had to walk her little sister Annie to Sunrise Elementary and drop her brother Paul off at Wedgewood Middle School.

"Hi," the boy said to Toya. He grinned and looked down at his sneakers when she smiled at him.

Paul was generally bold and outspoken, but Toya knew that he had a crush on her. But then again, who didn't?

"Where's Kim?" Serena asked her. "She's not coming with us?"

"No, she wasn't ready yet," Toya replied. "She gonna have to ride with Rick."

"You didn't want to ride with Rick?" Serena asked.

"Not really," Toya said. "Me and Mama were getting into it, and I didn't wanna stick around and listen to her mouth."

"What y'all getting into it about?"

"Mr. Sproles keeps reporting me absent. Mama said she talked to him. I don't know if he called her or if she called him."

Serena shook her head, smiling. "You do keep skipping his class, though."

"It's too late for him to be crying about that," Toya said. "We only have two weeks left in school. All I have to do is make a 50 on the final exam to pass his class. Why he care if I show up or not? They don't be doing nothing in his class anyway."

"Uh, maybe because skipping school is *wrong*," Serena offered.

The way she said it, Toya knew she was delivering the message more for her siblings' benefit.

"Yeah, you right," she said. "But sometimes he counts me absent even when I'm there."

Serena knew that wasn't the case, but she didn't contradict her friend. Toya was a perpetual bad apple, but she was right about one thing: They were both seniors, and their days at Finley High were surely numbered. If they didn't have their heads screwed on correctly by now, there was little Mr. Sproles or any other teacher could do to fix them at this point.

They walked in silence for a while, everyone in their own thoughts, until Serena's sister Sheila noticed a dark-colored Buick approaching from the opposite direction. The car slowed down as it neared them.

"Who's that?" Sheila wondered.

"Might be a driveby," Paul ventured.

Serena didn't like her brother's morbid sense of humor, but she couldn't deny that DANGER was the first thing on her mind as well. Even though no one in her group had wronged anyone – that she knew of – when you live in a bad neighborhood, trouble can find you just the same.

The hairs stood on the back of her neck when the car stopped in the middle of the street and the driver's window rolled down slowly. Serena saw that the man behind the wheel was a stranger who looked to be in his early thirties. She didn't know his name, but she thought she recognized him as one of the dope boys who made an illegal living in her neighborhood. Judging by his age and his flashy jewelry, she thought he might be a supplier for the local dealers. Either way, she knew this guy was bad news, much like a driveby, and she kept her feet moving.

"Hold up," the man said. "Can I holler at y'all for a second?"

"Nope!"

Serena increased her pace. She took hold of Sheila's hand and dragged her until she was moving faster as well. Paul remained curious, but he didn't slow down either.

"What you want?"

Serena looked back and was shocked to see Toya approaching the vehicle. She hesitated, not sure if she should leave her friend behind or wait for her. The high probability of danger had her eyes dilated. Now she feared for Toya's safety as much as she worried about her brother and sister. If she left her friend there, and Toya didn't show up for school, Serena didn't think she could live with the guilt.

She kept walking until she, Paul and Sheila were a safe distance away, and then she stopped and turned to wait on Toya. From twenty feet away, she couldn't hear every word that was said. But she could tell by the tone of the stranger's voice that he was flirting.

She shook her head in disappointment as Toya approached the vehicle with a sultry smile on her face. She leaned on the Buick's doorframe with her big booty poking out. Serena was seething by the time Toya plugged the creep's number into her phone and hurried to catch up with them. Serena saw the guy staring at her friend's physique in his side mirror before he slowly drove away.

"Alright, I'm ready," Toya said, totally oblivious to her friend's change in demeanor.

"What the hell is wrong with you?" Serena asked with a deep scowl marring her features.

"What?" Toya said. "I just wanted to see what he wanted."

"You know what he wanted," Serena grumbled as they got moving again. "He's a damned pervert."

Toya chuckled. "You don't know that."

"How come I don't? He sees some kids walking to school and decides to stop and holler at them? What kind of grown man does that?"

"I'm *nineteen*," Toya reminded her. "You saying I can't holler at somebody who's in their twenties?"

"Not if they know you're still in high school, but they want to talk to you anyway. That dude's a straight *molester*," Serena guessed.

"*Chester the molester*," Paul joked.

"Shut up," Serena told him. "This is serious."

"We graduate in two weeks," Toya repeated. "After that, we're adults. There's nothing wrong with a twenty-five year old man talking to a twenty year old woman. Hell, nobody cares if a forty year old man talks to a thirty year old woman."

Serena's eyes and mouth fell open at the same pace. She had a lot to tell her friend, but she let her mouth snap shut on the words. She'd known Toya since the sixth grade. When Toya decided she was right about something, it was nearly impossible to convince her otherwise. Usually it wasn't worth her time.

"You the one pregnant," Toya reminded her. "Don't look at me like I'm over here making bad life decisions."

Serena squeezed her eyes closed for a second. She saw red behind her eyelids. It was clear that she and Toya had to fight it out. There was no way around it. Some people had their heads stuck so far up their butt, they won't give you the respect you deserve until you fatten their lip.

But no – that was the old Serena talking. Her pregnancy was a huge wake up call. She'd taken steps to change her life ever since her EPT test came back positive. Serena was going to church now and planning for her and her baby's future. She was trying her best to leave her hoodrat ways behind.

Her friend Jamar warned that if she continued to hang around certain people from her past, she might get pulled back down with them. Serena didn't want to cut any of her old friends out of her life, but it was becoming increasingly obvious that she had no choice. It wasn't just her soul that was at stake. It was her baby's too.

But Toya surprised her by saying, "I'm sorry. I didn't mean to say that."

Serena shook her head. "Just forget it," she said, and the group continued on their way.

● ● ● ● ● ●

They dropped Annie off first and then Paul. As the two seniors made the final trek to Finley High, Toya's guilt started to weigh on her. She and Serena hadn't spoken to each other for over five minutes.

"Hey, I'm sorry, for real," she said. "I know I shouldn't have said that about you being pregnant – not in front of your brother and sister."

"Really? That's what you're sorry about?"

"Uh, yeah. Ain't that what you mad about?"

"I'm mad about everything," Serena revealed. "Why would you stop and talk to that man?"

"He's only twenty-three," Toya informed her.

"Yeah right. I'm sure he told you that *after* you told him how old you are."

Toya gave that some thought. She smacked her lips. "Even if he's twenty-five, I'll be out of high school next week. I can talk to whoever I want to."

"But you're not out *now*. What do you think goes through Sheila's head when she sees you doing something like that? Do you think I want her to stop for some random punk who's following her on the way to school?"

"No, I don't, Serena. I said my bad."

"Yeah, your bad for a lot of stuff."

Toya bristled. It wasn't in her nature to be this apologetic. The least Serena could do was humble herself.

"You know what, you been acting real funny, since you and Jamar started hanging out…"

Serena chuckled. Jamar was the founder of Finley High's bible club. He was also the boy who took Serena to the prom and later comforted her when her secret pregnancy became everybody's business.

"We don't have to hang out no more," she told her friend bluntly.

Toya rolled her eyes dismissively. "I didn't say all that. You just be acting different, that's all."

"I'm pregnant," Serena simply stated. "My life is changing. I have to change with it. I don't want my child to grow up and be like me – not the me I am right now – or the me I used to be."

Toya looked her in the eyes and nodded. "Alright. I understand that. And I'm sorry for talking to that guy in front of Sheila and Paul. You right. That wasn't cool."

Serena didn't know if she meant that, but it didn't matter. It was over, and there was no point in holding a grudge.

"It's fine," she said. "I'm not mad at you."

"Cool," Toya said.

The girls walked quietly for another few minutes until they reached their school. The courtyard was bustling with excited students; some chilling, some heading inside. Serena and Toya didn't have first period together. They regarded each other awkwardly when they entered the main building.

"Alright, well, I guess I'll see you later," Serena told her.

"Alright," Toya said. "See ya..."

CHAPTER THREE
TAKING NOTES

By the end of second period the disagreement Toya had with Serena was the last thing on her mind. She had plenty of admirers at school who could help her get through anything, from a fight with her mom to a failed test returned by a teacher.

In first period Sammy, the unofficial class clown, made like he wanted to grab Toya's butt when she passed him on the way to her seat in the back of the classroom. She cut her eyes at him and said, "*I wish you would,*" and his arm froze in the air, his hand still in the booty squeeze position.

"What?" he said. "I didn't do nothing."

"Don't play with me, boy," Toya said as she kept moving.

"Why you dressed like that, if you don't want nobody to touch you?" Sammy wanted to know.

Toya didn't have to look back to know that his eyes were glued to her curves and his smile was ear to ear.

She almost told him that her outfit was for him to *look* rather than *touch*, but she didn't want to give him free range to ogle her all day. Sammy was old enough to know a thirst trap when he saw it. If he was foolish enough to get ensnared in her web every morning, that was his problem.

Besides, Toya liked it when people were taken aback by her appearance. The brief commotion with Sammy caused all of the other boys in the classroom to look her way, and they were quickly enthralled as well. Even the Mexican boys couldn't stop themselves from shooting horny glances her way for the rest of the period. When the bell rang, at least ten students remained seated, so they could get a good view of Toya when she exited the classroom ahead of them.

By second period Toya was up to 120 "Likes" on the Facebook selfie she posted this morning. One of the boys who had commented on the pic, Travis Combs, tried to sit next to her, although Mr. Williams had assigned seating for his class.

"Hey," he said. "What's up, girl?"

"What's up?" Toya replied. She removed a spiral notebook and a pen from her backpack and placed it on her desktop, like a good girl.

"You still messing with Derrick?" Travis asked.

Toya's relationship status was common knowledge, so she didn't bother denying it, even though Travis was a cutie, and she'd always been interested in him.

Travis was one of those rare students who was smart and always a fashionable dresser, but he avoided hanging out with the jocks or any other popular clique. He wasn't a nerd, but he was a solid A/B student. As far as Toya knew, he never smoked weed or even skipped class.

"Yeah," she said, in response to his question. "Something like that."

Travis' head tilted slowly. "What that mean?" He wore his hair short and curly on top. His skin was the color of a sugar cookie.

Another student named Bethany approached them and told Travis, "Hey, this is my seat."

"Let's switch for today," he suggested.

Bethany looked to his seat at the front of the room and gave him a look of displeasure. But she wasn't the confrontational type, so she turned and headed that way.

"So, what that mean?" Travis asked Toya again. "You not with him anymore?"

Toya did consider herself to be in a relationship with Derrick. But since he was so cagey about their exclusiveness, she grinned and told Travis, "It's complicated."

Travis grinned too. He leaned back in his seat, in preparation for some big-time macking, but Mr. Williams wasn't having it.

"Bethany, why are you out of your seat?"

The girl's face reddened. She looked down at her desk, rather than snitch on another student.

"Travis," Mr. Williams said, "why are you not in *your* seat? Who told you and Bethany to switch seats today? You know what, I don't even want an answer. *I* didn't tell you to switch, so could both of you please return to your assigned seats?"

Travis didn't look Toya's way again as he stood to do as he was told. Bethany gave him an apologetic look as they passed each other in the aisle, as if this problem was her fault somehow.

When Mr. Williams' class ended, Toya got even more adulations from the crowd of students who packed the hallways each passing period. She never understood why women were offended by catcalls they received from construction workers and random losers. Who doesn't want to be told they're sexy and beautiful?

Before she made it to her locker, Toya heard a number of things, ranging from, "*Damn, girl,*" to "*When you gon' let me hit that?*" which made her feel superior to all of the ugly chicks who got ignored.

Derrick stopped by her locker wearing long, Dickey shorts and a tee-shirt. Considering how important fashion is in high school, Toya would've considered his outfit *subpar*. But he also wore a pair of $250 Nike sneakers that made up for everything else. He was a tall kid with dark skin and a head full of dreadlocks.

He was one of the star players for Finley High's basketball team, and it was his hair that first attracted Toya. When Derrick hustled on the court, his shoulder-length dreads would fly to and fro. He had to wear a headband to keep them out of his eyes. Derrick wasn't good enough to get a scholarship to any university, but he planned to try out for TCU and Texas Lutheran and hopefully prove their scouts wrong.

"Hey, girl." He leaned against the locker adjacent to Toya's while she looked for her biology notebook.

"Here." She handed him her backpack so she could free up both hands.

"What you looking for?" Derrick asked her. "You know you don't be doing no work."

"Who you talking about?" Toya asked him. "You the one who only passes during basketball season. Are you even graduating?"

"Probably," Derrick said. "I'm waiting to get my score from that last test. I see you wore those leggings, like I told you to," he noticed.

He looked her up and down unabashedly while Toya continued to busy herself in her locker. She pretended not to notice.

"I didn't wear nothing for you," she quipped. "I wear whatever I want."

"Yeah, but I'm the one who told you to wear those today."

"You not the only one who likes seeing me in these pants."

"Why you gotta run your mouth all the time?" he asked.

His tone sounded serious, but when Toya looked over at him, she saw that he was smiling.

"I can say whatever I want to," she told him. "If you was my man, then maybe things would be different..."

Derrick didn't take the bait. Why be her boyfriend when he could get the benefits without the commitment?

"Are you coming to my house at lunch?"

She shook her head. "Nope."

"Why not?"

"Because I'm hungry, and you don't never have no food there."

"I can get you something to eat," he said right away. "We can stop by McDonald's."

"I'm not paying for no McDonald's."

"I'll pay for it," Derrick said, unaware that he was already fully immersed in a pattern of behavior that would remain the same for the rest of his life: When it comes to women, you gotta pay before you play.

Toya looked him in the eyes. Her skin was cocoa brown, her lips naturally pink with no gloss. Her hair was past her shoulders. Her real hair barely reached her neckline. Finding a donor to pay for her extensions was a challenge, but she always pulled through.

"Alright. I'll think about it."

Derrick tried not to show how excited he was.

"Bet."

"Think about what?" someone said at the same moment.

Toya turned and beamed when she saw her bestie. Her clique at school consisted of four friends – well more like three now, since Serena was acting funny. But even when there were four, Cicely had always been Toya's favorite running buddy. She knew Toya's heart like no other.

"Girl, what's up!" Toya gave her a big hug. "Derrick wants me to go to his house at lunchtime. You wanna go? He said he'll take us to McDonald's."

Derrick's eyes widened for a moment, but he didn't contradict her.

"I don't know," Cicely said, looking over her friend's shoulder. She loved to kick it with Toya, but she had her own crush to consider.

"I'll buy you a combo meal," Derrick offered. "Both of y'all."

He immediately hated that he offered. It wasn't about the money. It was about him trying too hard. He viewed his eagerness as a weakness.

A lot of the kids in the noisy hallway started to get a move on, some outright running, and Toya knew that she'd better get to class too.

"I'll talk to you later." She took her backpack and turned her back on Derrick (who was very happy that she turned her back on him).

I hate to see you leave, but...

"Alright. I'll meet you here next period," he called, but Toya and Cicely were too far away to hear him then. They were huddled together, walking and snickering.

Derrick walked away snickering, too.

● ● ● ● ● ●

Cicely and Toya sat next to each other in Mrs. Peete's third period biology class. They couldn't talk outright, but due to the fact that they were sitting at a lab table rather than desks, they were able to have a running conversation on their spiral notebooks. Toya wrote on hers, and Cicely wrote on hers.

Mrs. Peete saw them writing, but she thought they were taking notes on her boring lecture. She stayed up all night working on her lesson plan. She really thought she was in the zone.

You coming with me to Derrick's? Toya wrote.

No, Cicely scribbled.

Why not?

It stink over there

Toya had to fight to stop her smile from birthing a burst of laughter. It did stink at Derrick's house. He had six brothers and sisters in a three bedroom flat. Even Martha

35

Stewart would've thrown in the towel, if she was the mama over there.

Come anyway

Why?

Toya looked up at her friend and gave her a quick smile. Cicely was very pretty. Toya would admit that Cicely was prettier than she was, but only in her mind – never out loud. Cicely was taller, with a slim face and sharp features. She had a body like an upscale model. But that body was where Toya took the lead, in her opinion. Meghan Trainor said boys like a little more booty to hold at night. Toya found that to be true.

Because I don't wanna go by myself. We can smoke some weed

Cicely looked up at her and grinned. Smoking weed was definitely something she was interested in, but she didn't have to go with Toya to do that. She was pretty sure her boyfriend already had a blunt waiting for her.

She wrote, **I can smoke with Byron at lunch. If you scared, stay here**

But I wanna go, Toya wrote, and she cracked a smile. Cicely told her, **You nasty**

And you're a virgin? Not! You did it before me **No I didn't!**

Yes you did!

Cicely shook her head. She couldn't stop from chuckling. Toya had been giving it up since the sixth grade.

At least Cicely waited until she made it to high school. She looked up and Mrs. Peete was staring right at her.

"Are you paying attention?"

Cicely's ears burned. "Yes, Ma'am."

The teacher had only to walk over and look down at their notebooks to know for sure. If she did that, Mrs. Peete would retrieve enough evidence to prove that the girls had been skipping school. She could also get Cicely and Toya in trouble at home for their drug use and promiscuity. But she didn't get paid enough to go through all of that.

Instead she gave Cicely a look that said, "*I got my eye on you – my **good** one,*" and continued with her lecture.

Cicely waited a full minute before she wrote, I'm not going. I already got in trouble with my mama

Why? What happened?

Skipping

Toya shook her head. Teachers were the ultimate snitches.

Take Sandra, Cicely suggested.

Toya wrote, *She scary too*

Two scardy cats are better than one

Toya grinned and flipped to the middle of her notebook. She looked up and gave their teacher as much attention as she could muster, thus ending the conversation.

CHAPTER FOUR
LEFT OUT

People say love is all you need
Like a warm, gentle breeze
It puts you at ease
Like a mother's smile
It can make you joyous
But for me, I think love is poisonous

When the class ended, the students waited anxiously for Mrs. Peete to dismiss them, because she was on a power trip, and she'd make you stay even later if you jumped up at the sound of the bell.

When they finally made it out of the room, Cicely and Toya encountered the third member of their crew headed for the lockers.

"Hey, what's up!"

Cassandra, typically referred to as Sandra, rushed to them, her smile sunny and wide. As far as looks went, Sandra was often considered the least attractive member of their group, though this was hardly the case. She had rich, dark skin and big, beautiful brown eyes. Rather than her appearance, it was her reserved nature that allowed her friends to outshine her.

Sandra's mom would have an aneurysm if she tried to leave for school in some of the outfits Toya wore on a regular basis – not that Sandra wanted to dress like that. She was fine with hanging out in her friends' shadows. She got in a lot less trouble that way.

"Girl, where you been?" Toya asked her as the trio headed for her locker.

"In class," Sandra said. "Where you think?"

"I was looking for you this morning."

"My mama was running late," Sandra explained. "I had to go straight to class when I got here. What's going on with Mrs. Peete today?" She didn't have biology until 7th period. Sometimes it was helpful to know what to expect.

"Ooh, girl you might wanna find you some caffeine pills," Cicely told her. "She didn't do nothing but lecture the whole time."

"Yeah, I wouldn't have made it without Cicely," Toya tacked on. "Ain't you in there by yourself?"

"No, Serena's in there with me," Sandra told her.

"Me and her got into it today," Toya said as she opened her locker.

Her two friends flanked her.

"Why, what happened?" Sandra asked.

"You know she been acting funny," Toya quipped.

"You shouldn't have told everybody she was pregnant," Cicely stated.

"You shouldn't have told *me* she was pregnant," Toya replied. "You know I can't keep a secret."

The girls laughed, and then Cicely noticed a group of cute boys heading their way.

"Here come your man," she told Toya.

Toya looked back and saw that Derrick had returned as promised. No surprise there. She could've told him to meet her on the moon, and he would've found a way to make it.

"Hey, you ready?"

Toya tossed her backpack into her locker and then turned to face him. Derrick brought two friends with him. Chris and Rodney were members of the school's basketball team. Rodney also played varsity football. Chris did double-duty as well on the school's track team. He ran the last leg on the 4 by 400 relay squad. Everyone knew him as the fastest student at Finley High.

Altogether the three boys were tall, dark and scrumptious. If popularity paid a salary, they would be millionaires.

Derrick approached Toya and placed both hands on her hips. She pushed him away, but he didn't let go. He pulled her into his arms, and both of his hands quickly made their way to her plump derriere. She pushed him again, more forcefully this time.

"Boy, stop!"

He let go, and she backed up against her locker. She was smiling, and Derrick was too. Their friends watched their interaction with amused and envious expressions. Rodney was jealous because after three years of flirting, Toya never gave him any play. Sandra was green-eyed because she longed for a boy who would want her as much as Derrick wanted Toya. The problem was she wasn't sure how to obtain that goal without giving up too much of herself.

"Come on. You ready?" Derrick took hold of Toya's hand and pulled her away from the locker.

The crowd in the hallway began to thin out as most of the students hurried to lunch or to their fourth period class.

"Wait," Toya said. She looked back at her friends. "Cicely, you coming, right?"

"Where y'all going?" Sandra asked.

"To Derrick's house," Toya told her. "You wanna come with us?"

Sandra checked out the boys again. She looked away, grinning coyly. The jocks all looked nearly grown. She knew they were looking for some grown folk activities to get involved in.

"Come on, Cicely," Toya begged.

Her friend hesitated. "I gotta–"

Her boyfriend Byron stepped to them, seemingly out of nowhere, and wrapped her up in a hug from behind. Cicely frowned for a second and then settled into his embrace when she realized who it was.

"I been looking for you," Byron said, his lips close to her ear. He kissed her sweet-smelling neck. Cicely's eyes fluttered in a sea of bliss. Her smile was soft and content.

Byron was good-looking and popular. He had short hair and he wore glasses, but he wasn't smart enough to be considered a nerd. He was a frontrunner when it came to fashion on campus. He was fair-skinned with a nearly perfect goatee.

Cicely placed her hands over Byron's and told Toya, "I'm not going."

This time there was no point in trying to talk her out of it. Whenever Byron was in the picture, he was always Cicely's first choice. Not even her best friends could compete with him.

41

Once again Sandra felt like a third wheel as she watched her friends with their boyfriends. She hated to feel left out, especially while she was seemingly in the midst of everything. She didn't have a steady boyfriend at the moment or even a serious crush.

"Sandra, you coming?" Toya asked again. "Derrick said he'll buy us lunch."

Sandra hesitated. She'd gone out to lunch with Toya and her boyfriend before, and it wasn't all that great. Derrick's house was cluttered and funky. And contrary to Toya's beliefs, Sandra didn't find any amusement in watching her make-out for thirty minutes.

"Come on. Chris is coming, too," Derrick said, as if reading her mind.

Sandra looked up at Chris. He was so fine, her heart sighed when he looked her in the eyes.

"Yeah, come with us," Chris said.

He had dark, curly hair and light brown eyes. His feats on the basketball court and track field were legendary at the school. Sandra knew of at least three girls he had sex with. One of them was Rosalyn James, the prettiest cheerleader on the squad. Sandra couldn't believe she was so close to being with someone Rosalyn had been with. Just thinking about it made her stomach shudder with excited butterflies.

"Okay, I'll go," she decided.

Chris grinned. Rodney frowned.

"I guess y'all just gon' leave me stuck out," he deduced.

"Hell yeah you gon' be stuck out," Byron said, "if you thought you was finna kick it with *my* girl..."

Cicely was surprised to hear her boyfriend stand up to the jocks like that, especially since he didn't have anyone on his side to help him if they decided to get an attitude. Byron's courage and defense of her honor warmed and melted her heart. She turned to give him a kiss.

"I love you," she said when their lips separated.

"Love you too, baby."

The couple walked off hand in hand, and Rodney walked off by his lonesome.

Derrick asked his group, "Y'all ready to go?"

They all agreed that they were.

CHAPTER FIVE
UP IN SMOKE

A boyfriend who is boisterous and bold
One of the most courageous guys I know
Because he protects me
Like a guard dog, you know?
But even with all this protection
It might be borderline obsession

Derrick drove a 2001 Camry. It was a four-door, so Sandra and Chris were relatively comfortable in the back, while Derrick and Toya occupied the front seats. The car was surprisingly clean, given the haphazard nature of high school seniors. But it did have a lingering odor of cigarette smoke and old gym clothes. Sandra didn't mind the smell. She barely noticed it because she was trying hard not to look at Chris and let on how nervous she was.

They left the school with no problem. There was a security guard manning the parking lot's exit, but Derrick had a sticker on his windshield that identified him as a senior with privileges to leave for lunch. The security officer did approach the vehicle, to make sure all of the other occupants were seniors.

He told the teens to, "Be careful out there," as they rolled by.

There was a McDonald's restaurant within a few blocks of the school. When they got there, Derrick made good on his promise to feed both of the girls. Toya ordered the Double Quarter Pounder meal. Sandra said she'd have the same.

"I just want a chicken sandwich!" Derrick yelled at the drive-thru speaker.

"Would you like fries or a drink with that?"

"Naw."

He turned in his seat to look at Chris. "You want something?"

He shrugged. "Yeah. I guess I'll take the number ten."

Derrick relayed the order. When they got to the next window, he seemed surprised to find only one ten dollar bill in his wallet. He turned to Chris again.

"Hey, you got nine dollars?"

Chris frowned. "Mine was only five dollars."

"You can help pay for these girls," Derrick complained.

Chris balked at the notion, but he reached into his pocket and produced the funds. Toya snickered at their banter, but Sandra began to feel self-conscious again. She didn't like to be a burden. She was so uncomfortable by then, she barely had an appetite. But Toya began to stuff French fries into her mouth the moment she got her bag, so Sandra did the same. Making the guys pay for her meal was bad enough. Making them pay for food she wasn't going to eat would be even worse.

After leaving the restaurant, Derrick headed straight for his house, which was only a couple of miles away from the school. Finley High wasn't in a bad neighborhood, but it wasn't a great neighborhood, either. It was one of those rare areas where you could find hundred thousand dollar homes and crack houses within a mile radius.

Derrick lived closer to the crack houses.

He pulled into his driveway and hopped out with a pep in his step. He had already devoured his chicken sandwich, and Toya was mostly done with her food. She slurped the last of her soda through the straw before leaving the cup and her bag in the car.

"Bring that stuff with you," Derrick told her. "Don't be getting my car all junky."

"You want me to bring more trash in your house?" Toya joked. "Don't y'all have enough in there already?"

"Man, shut up," Derrick told her. "Always complaining. Just get that stuff out my car, like I said."

Sandra was surprised to hear him talk to her like that. He was all sugar and spice when they were at school. Now that he had Toya where he wanted her, apparently he felt comfortable enough to be himself.

Sandra made eye contact with her friend when Toya ducked back into the car to get her trash. Sandra looked a little apprehensive, but Toya was smiling, so she didn't say anything.

"You through eating?" Chris asked as Sandra unfastened her safety belt.

It was the first thing he had said to her since they left the school.

"I'm almost done," she told him.

"Why you can't look me in the eyes?" he asked her. "You scared?"

46

Sandra's mouth was extremely dry. She took a sip of her soda before she looked up at him. She shook her head. "No."

"You pretty," Chris told her. "I don't think I ever noticed you before."

His straw-colored eyes were absolutely dreamy. Sandra found herself getting lost in them. She couldn't believe he was looking at her, with those eyes. He smiled, and she had to look away again. Her whole body felt heated.

"Y'all getting out the car, or what?" Derrick wanted to know. He had to step over a rather large puddle of oil that hadn't fully seeped into his gravel driveway.

"Yeah," Chris shouted to him. He asked Sandra, "You ready?"

She didn't know what she was agreeing to, but she nodded and followed him out of the car.

● ● ● ● ● ●

Derrick's home was as deplorable as Sandra remembered it. She had only been there one other time. She'd vowed to never come back, out of fear that a roach might crawl up her leg if she let her guard down. But Chris made her forget about little incidentals like that.

The carpet in the living room was threadbare and visibly stained in numerous places. It was dark brown, but Sandra thought a steam cleaner might reveal the carpet's true beige hue. There was an old TV in the front room that still had a fat back and two couches that didn't match. Both sofas had a few items of clothing draped over the back or on the seat cushions. Derrick nonchalantly pushed the debris to the side before he and Toya sat down.

Sandra was disgusted to find a gnawed chicken bone on the sofa she and Chris were left with. She tried not to let on how upset she was, about the whole scene, but her stomach twisted, and she thought she might throw up.

"Man, what the hell?" Chris whined. "Y'all nasty asses can't even throw away a damned chicken bone?"

Toya laughed at that. Derrick didn't make any moves to remedy the situation.

"Dog, just move it out the way," he advised him.

"I don't wanna touch it," Chris said, his features set in a sneer.

"Say, you acting like a straight up punk right about now," Derrick told him. "I don't go to your house talking noise. I *definitely* wouldn't do it if you had a girl with you."

"That's 'cause my house ain't funky like yours," Chris responded. "Y'all using sheets for curtains," he said, looking around the room. "Your house is *grimey*, my dude."

Sandra was surprised to hear Chris clowning his friend like that. And she was grateful, because he was saying everything she was thinking. But she hoped the argument wouldn't escalate. Boys were known to have quick tempers when they knew girls were watching. Luckily Derrick proved to be more horny than upset.

He stood and helped Toya to her feet.

"Come on," he told her. "Let's go to my room. Y'all can sit over here," he told Chris and Sandra.

Toya shot Sandra a look before she and Derrick disappeared down the hallway. Sandra knew her friend well, but she couldn't read her eyes at that moment. Toya looked happy, but she also looked wary. She was definitely more excited than anxious.

As the couple walked away, Sandra and Chris moved to the spot they vacated. Sandra noticed Chris watching Toya's butt before they sat down. Derrick looked back, and he noticed, too.

"Say, don't be looking at my woman like that," he warned.

"I ain't your woman," Toya quipped.

"Yeah, but this is mines," Derrick said, and he fondled her bubble butt openly.

Toya kept walking, without pushing his hand away.

Emboldened, Derrick looked back at Chris and grinned before he reached with both hands and suddenly yanked her stretch pants down past her hips. Sandra was stunned to get a glimpse of her friend's panties. She was even more surprised when Toya made no moves to stop him. She simply made a right and disappeared into the last room in the hallway. Derrick gave his buddy a quick, conspiratorial nod before he followed her and then closed the door.

Sandra felt perspiration on her forehead when Chris turned back to her. Her heart was beating so fast, she knew she wouldn't finish her leftover burger and fries. She placed the McDonald's bag on the cushion to her right. She looked around, but there was no coffee table to sit her drink on. She placed it on the floor between her feet instead.

"They crazy," Chris said.

He smiled at her. Sandra had to force herself to smile back.

"So, um, what's up with you?" he asked her.

Sandra's eyes darted. She sat with her hands in her lap. She felt sweat on her palms. She tried to look casual as she wiped her hands on her thighs, hoping her jeans would absorb the moisture.

"Your, uh, your name's Cassandra, right?"

She nodded, though she considered that an odd question. She and Chris had been going to the same school for four years. Surely he knew her name.

He waited a few beats and then asked, "Do you like school?"

Sandra found that question even more peculiar than the other one.

Do I like school?

That's the type of thing you'd ask someone when you had absolutely nothing to say to that person.

"Yes," she told him. "It's alright."

"You make good grades, huh?"

Sandra nodded. She wasn't a straight A student, but she didn't fail classes or make very many C's, unlike her friends Toya and Cicely.

Chris nodded. He watched her for a few moments, as if waiting for her to expound on her response. But Sandra didn't have anything else to say. Chris yawned, and then he dug in his McDonald's bag for a few chicken nuggets he had left. He stared at the blank television screen while he ate. Sandra rubbed her hands on her pants again. She looked around uneasily. She thought the awkwardness of their conversation was mostly Chris' fault, because he was the one asking yes or no questions.

To make matters worse, it didn't take long before sounds from the back room began to make their way to the front of the house.

Sex sounds.

At first Sandra hoped Derrick was giving her friend a massage. A *really* good one. But after a minute the moaning was accompanied by the sound of a mattress squeaking, and Sandra knew Toya was being freaky again.

Her eyes widened when Chris cocked his head and then looked at her. He grinned. He was very handsome, but Sandra found herself growing more and more wary of him. She didn't know why. She didn't think he would cause her any harm, but the whole vibe of their lunch date was not right. She wasn't sure what she thought it would be, but this wasn't it.

"Damn," Chris said with a chuckle. "They getting it in..."

Sandra swallowed. Was that something she should respond to? What would she say?

Yeah, they sure are! Hardy har har!

The scene took another strange turn when Chris leaned in suddenly to kiss her. Sandra knew something along those lines was coming. She was not opposed to kissing Chris, but he bypassed her lips and left her puckered up for nothing. Instead he kissed her on the neck. Still, the sensation of his lips on her hot flesh made her feel tingly all over.

Chris kissed and sucked everything from her earlobe to her collar bone, while Sandra listened to Toya's sex sounds and stared at Derrick's filthy house. As much as she liked Chris, she knew this wasn't right. She couldn't force her mind to get in the mood. She closed her eyes, hoping that would help.

Unaware of her mental anguish, Chris quickly transitioned to second base. He brought a hand up and touched and then caressed her chest. Sandra gasped. Her eyelids popped open, and her chest began to heave with her heavy breaths.

Egged on by her panting (which could only mean she was lusting for him), Chris' hand moved from her chest to her stomach and finally between her legs. He hated that she was wearing jeans rather than stretch pants, like Toya. He couldn't feel anything through those jeans. As a matter of fact, Chris hated that Sandra *wasn't* Toya. But when you're eighteen, a piece of tail is a piece of tail, and it was almost always worth it.

Except sometimes it wasn't.

Sandra abruptly pulled away and pushed his hand out of her lap.

"Wait. Stop."

She was flustered. She looked hot and bothered. But if that was the case, why was she stopping him? Chris didn't understand. Was she rejecting him? Surely she didn't think she would ever find a better guy. It's not like she was the belle of the ball.

"We don't, we don't really know each other," she managed.

You just asked my name two minutes ago!

Chris sighed inwardly. He was young, but he had experienced this before. Some girls required you to kick it with them for a while before they would give it up. Some chicks wouldn't get down unless they were intoxicated. He thought he knew a way to accomplish both of these goals simultaneously.

He reached into his pocket and produced a small baggie filled with marijuana. From his other pocket came a skinny cigar that was in miraculously good shape, considering he'd been sitting in the car and then on the couch for the past twenty minutes.

He proceeded to roll a blunt with a quickness and finesse that made it clear this wasn't his first, second or third time doing so. He didn't notice the look of indifference on Sandra's face until he lit it, took a drag and foolishly offered it to her.

He pulled back when she frowned.

"You don't smoke?"

She shook her head.

Chris sighed in both disbelief and frustration. He took another drag from the cigar and was courteous enough to blow the smoke in the opposite direction. He couldn't believe Derrick hooked him up with such a loser. He considered his next move and quickly realized he didn't have one. He and Sandra were clearly not on the same page.

"So, ain't nothing going down, huh?" he asked bluntly.

Sandra didn't want to upset him, but she couldn't imagine herself having sex with someone who didn't know her or even care to get to know her. She definitely wasn't going to smoke weed and return to school high. She didn't understand how he could do that, either. Chris was the star of the track team, for God's sake! Everything Sandra knew about smoking taught her that it was particularly bad for your lungs – two very important organs, when it came to running track.

She cleared her throat and shook her head again.

She didn't know what to expect after that. She was caught off guard when Chris stood unexpectedly and returned his drugs to the front pocket of his jeans.

"I'm finna bounce," he declared. "Tell Derrick I'll holler at him later."

Sandra thought he was kidding, but Chris proceeded to walk to the front door and exit the house, still puffing his Mary Jane.

Sandra sat quietly for a few minutes until the humping sounds from the back room began to get louder and louder. Or maybe she only imagined they were louder. Whatever the case, Sandra found herself going crazy as she sat there on that disgusting couch. The sight of a pregnant roach scaling an adjacent wall finally got her moving.

She was depressed and rejected. She couldn't fight off these emotions, but she didn't have to feel that way inside a roach motel.

By the time she got outside, Chris was nowhere in sight. That was perfect. Sandra had to walk nearly two miles back to school. In her current state of mind, that was something she preferred to do alone.

CHAPTER SIX
GOING NOWHERE FAST

Sandra didn't catch up with her friends until after school. When she approached Toya's locker, her friends were speaking quietly, giggling. Sandra felt self-conscious when they turned to acknowledge her, though she knew they were probably talking about boys rather than her.

"Girl, where you been?" Toya exclaimed. "Why you didn't answer my texts?"

Sandra had received several text messages from her friend since lunchtime. Initially Toya wanted to know why she left Derrick's house. Later she sounded concerned about whether Sandra made it back to school safely.

"I didn't wanna talk about it through text messages," Sandra said sourly.

"What's wrong?" Cicely asked. Her face was filled with concern. "Did something happen with Chris? He did something to you?"

Sandra shook her head. "No. He tried to."

"What happened?" Toya asked. "Derrick told me Chris said you was acting funny."

Sandra sighed. She wasn't surprised the story was already spreading around the school.

"He started smoking," she explained. "And I didn't want to."

"Why not?" Toya asked.

"You know I don't smoke."

"Yeah, but you could have," Toya stated. "Don't you like Chris? That boy is *fine*."

"He is, but..." She searched Cicely's eyes for help with this.

"You don't have to smoke to be with somebody," Cicely said. "You don't have to act like somebody you're not."

Sandra was relieved that at least one of her friends understood her.

"What was he smoking?" Cicely asked. "Cigarettes or weed?"

"*Weed*."

"I smelled it when I came out," Toya said. "It smelled like some good."

"I didn't know Chris be smoking," Cicely commented.

"I didn't, either," Sandra told them.

"Did y'all at least get to do anything before you left?" Toya asked.

Sandra's face flushed with heat. Thankfully her skin tone was too dark to reveal this.

"Ooh! *You did!*" Cicely said. "You gotta tell us about it."

"Okay," Sandra said. "Where y'all about to go?"

"I don't know. Get into something," Toya said. "Maybe the mall..."

"Hey, Serena!" Cicely called.

56

The girls turned and saw their fourth running buddy heading their way. Technically Serena didn't hang with them enough nowadays to be considered their *running buddy*, but Sandra still considered her one of her best friends.

"Hey, what y'all doing?" Serena asked them.

She looked really nice today. She was a little over three months pregnant, but she wasn't showing yet. Sandra wondered if the pregnancy was the reason she was glowing.

Serena was walking with two other girls; a set of Hispanic twins named Rachel and Anna. The twins were in their graduating class, but they were not in Sandra's circle of friends. She had never seen Serena hang around them, either.

"Hey, twinkies," Cicely said, apparently in reference to the twins.

"Hi." The girls spoke at the same time.

"What y'all getting into?" Cicely asked them. "We're thinking about catching the bus to the mall. You wanna go?" she asked Serena.

"Nah, we're working on a project for Ms. Meredith," Serena said. "I'll have to catch up with y'all some other time."

"Alright, that's cool," Cicely said. "Y'all have fun too, I guess..."

Everyone was all smiles until Serena and the twins continued on their way.

"*Twinkies?*" Toya said with a frown. "What the hell does that mean?"

"Oh the twins," Cicely said with a chuckle. "That's what people call them, the twinkies."

Toya shook her head in annoyance. "Why is Serena hanging around them? How do *you* even know them?"

"They go to Jamar's bible meetings," Cicely explained.

"That's lame," Toya said.

"Why don't you go to those meetings anymore?" Sandra asked Cicely.

"Because she'd rather be sucking on Byron's tongue at lunchtime," Toya said with a cackle.

Cicely couldn't contradict that. She laughed as well.

● ● ● ● ● ●

"We're gonna catch the bus."

Sandra spoke into her cellphone while her friends stood watching her. They had already made it to the bus stop, so she hoped her mother wouldn't rain on her parade.

"What are y'all gonna do at the mall?" Dorothy asked. "I know those girls don't have any money."

"They have enough to get something to eat at the food court. We won't be there that long."

"You don't have to go all the way to the mall to get something to eat."

"I know, Mama. We just wanted to, you know, hang out."

"Cassandra, y'all better not be in there stealing. Those girls *steal*. You keep hanging around them, you'll end up putting something in your purse, too. And you know I'm not having it..."

"I'm not, Mama." She looked up at Toya and Cicely. "They're not, either."

"Alright, but I gotta go to work tonight, and I want you home before I leave," her mother said. "I'll come pick you up at six-thirty."

"Okay," Sandra said with a smile.

"I'll call you when I'm on my way."

"Alright. Bye."

"Love you."

"Love you too, Mama. Bye."

Sandra disconnected and returned the phone to her back pocket. She told her friends, "She said I can go, but I have to leave at six-thirty."

"Cool," Cicely said. It was three-thirty, so that left them a good amount of time to kick it. She dug in her purse until she found a skinny joint and a lighter. She lit it up and blew a plume of smoke into the afternoon breeze.

"We're right down the street from the school," Sandra cautioned her.

"Yeah, but we're not *at* school," Cicely commented. "School's out. They can't do nothing, even if they do see me."

Toya wasn't concerned about her getting caught, either. "What did your mom say about us?" she asked Sandra, "when you said, '*they're not either?*'"

"She said she didn't want me to get in any trouble," Sandra said, wanting to spare her friends' feelings.

"Tell us what happened with you and Chris," Cicely said as she took a seat on the plastic bench the city provided for the bus stop. This one had a roof and three walls, so it was considered top of the line.

"*Heeeey!*" Toya yelled, waving at two students across the street.

It was Deshaun and Henry, a junior and senior who lived close enough to walk home. The boys waved, and then Henry shouted something, and they both laughed.

"*Okay!*" Toya yelled as she watched them turn the corner and disappear from sight. Her smile was big and toothy. "What'd he say?" she asked Cicely.

Her friend was surprised by the question. "You didn't hear him?"

Toya shook her head. "Uh-uhn."

"Then what'd you agree to it for?" Cicely wondered. "Talking about, '*Okay*'..."

Sandra shook her head, giggling.

"What'd he say?" Toya asked again.

"He said, '*When you gon' come home with me?*'" Sandra reported.

"Oh," Toya said. Her smile didn't falter. "Anyway, hurry up and tell us about Chris, before the bus gets here."

"Here," Cicely said, offering her the joint.

"Where'd you get this from?" Toya wondered. "Why it's so little?" She took the joint and took a long drag.

"It was all Derrick had left," Cicely said. "I rolled it myself." She beamed with pride.

Sandra sat next to Cicely and told them what happened with Chris. When she was done, her friends had plenty of unsolicited advice.

"You should've done it," Toya said.

"You know I don't smoke."

"I'm not talking about smoking," Toya said, returning the joint to Cicely. "I'm talking about when he kissed you. Why'd you push his hand away?"

"We didn't really kiss," Sandra explained. "He kissed me on my neck. I thought he was going to kiss me on my lips, but he didn't."

"My mama said boys won't kiss you on the lips, unless they really like you," Cicely offered.

"Yeah, that makes me feel better," Sandra said sarcastically.

"But you don't really like him, either," Cicely continued. "So what difference does it make?" She was careful not to blow any smoke in her friend's direction.

Sandra shrugged. "It's just... I don't know."

"You don't think he's fine?" Cicely wondered.

"I do," Sandra said right away.

"He's fine as hell," Toya agreed.

"You had a chance to be with him," Cicely said. "If he's so fine, why'd you back down?"

"I didn't have a chance to *be with him*. I had a chance to have sex."

"Yeah, same difference," Cicely said and laughed. "You don't want to have sex with him? I would have – I mean, if I wasn't with Byron."

"You still would have," Toya claimed. She took the joint from her. "If Byron didn't come and drag you off, you would've knocked Chris down *today*."

"No I wouldn't. I love Byron."

"You don't even know what love is," Toya stated.

"He didn't know my name," Sandra reiterated.

"So what?" Toya said. "You could've reminded him while y'all were getting it in. What are you trying to do, have a *relationship*?"

"No," Sandra said. There was no other way to answer that question when it was presented like that. "But dang, I do want him to at least *like* me."

"But you do want to have sex?" Cicely clarified. "You're not trying to be a born-again virgin, are you?"

"No," Sandra said and grinned. "I do want to have sex."

Her friends knew that Sandra's two sexual experiences had been rushed and unsatisfying. Both incidents were with a boyfriend, but the settings were all wrong. The first time was in Nick's mother's car in the driveway of his home. It was near sunset but not properly dark outside. Nick's whole family was in the house at the time, which made the threat of them getting caught more palpable than the actual sex.

The second time was with Brian, at the swimming pool in his apartment complex. It was dark that time, and the beach cot was less cramped than the backseat of Nick's mother's car. But humping outside, in an area Sandra was not totally comfortable with, was not an ideal scenario either.

"I want my next time to be in a *bed*," Sandra revealed. "With some privacy. I want to have time to, you know, take our time."

She expected her friends to balk at that notion. She was half right.

"What you want, some rose petals on the floor, too?" Toya joked.

Sandra rolled her eyes.

Cicely said, "There's nothing wrong with that. That's what I be wanting with Byron. I wish we had somewhere we could go where we wouldn't have to worry about anybody bothering us. I can't wait until he moves out and gets his own apartment."

"That's why I'm glad Derrick lives so close," Toya boasted. "We can have the house all to ourselves at lunchtime. We lay in bed and smoke after we bone."

"But you too scared to go over there by yourself," Cicely noted, and they all laughed.

"What about the weed though?" Toya asked Sandra. "You'll be out of high school in two weeks. You ain't never gon' smoke?"

"Put that out. There's the bus," Cicely told her.

Toya tossed the joint on the grass behind the bus stop and blew out the last of her smoke.

"I don't know," Sandra said as she rose to her feet.

"It won't hurt to try it, right?" Toya said to Cicely.

"You're gonna end up smoking one day," Cicely predicted. "Everybody is. But you were right not to do it before you went back to school. You have to be a *real* smoker like me to come back high without anybody knowing it. Everybody can smell it, and the teachers be looking at your eyes. They can tell if you're high."

Sandra agreed with that, and it made her wonder about Chris again. How had he managed to accomplish so much at school if he smoked weed regularly? How did his coaches not know he was getting high?

"You think you'll have sex with Chris if he tries again?" Toya asked, reading her mind.

"Maybe," Sandra said as the bus came to a squeaky stop in front of them.

Cicely looked back and grinned at her sneaky smile. "Mmm-hmm," she said. "You want that boy."

Sandra didn't reply to that. Now that she'd gotten over the initial shock of his approach, she decided she would like another shot with him. Unfortunately she was pretty sure the popular jock would never give her the time of day again.

CHAPTER SEVEN
DELIQUENTS

Why should we love when we can hate?
Why build her up when we can break?
Why should we ask when we can take?
Clear 'em out and clean the slate
This is the life we choose to live
Can't stop it now, this train is rolling
This life is going, faster now
Spitting sparks. This train is stolen!

-KTW

When they got to the mall, Sandra was not surprised to hear that her friends had only five bucks between them, which, contrary to what she'd told her mom, was not enough for them to buy a meal at the food court. Lucky for them, Sandra had sixteen dollars in her purse. She offered to pay the difference, if the girls decided they did want to get something to eat.

In the meantime, they didn't need any money for their mall activities. They mostly just walked and talked and flirted with any cute boys who were bold enough to speak after looking their way. Sandra didn't realize it, but her threesome created an intimidating force, both for boys and girls.

"I can't stand these scary punks," Toya grumbled after a boy she had given the green light to smiled and walked away, rather than come and ask for her number.

"Who you talking about?" Cicely asked.

"Him," Toya said, gesturing towards a stranger who looked to be around their age.

"What'd he do?"

"Nothing," Toya said. "That's the problem. I don't see why he's staring, if he don't wanna say nothing."

"Byron said he was scared to walk up to me, when he first saw me with y'all," Cicely offered. "He waited until he could catch me by myself, before he asked for my number."

"How come?" Sandra asked. "Did he say why?"

"He said he thought he might get clowned," Cicely reported. "If I shot him down, he said he could take it from just me. But if I shot him down in front of y'all, it would've been too embarrassing."

"Derrick said he waited to get me by myself, too," Toya told them. "But his reason was different."

"What was his reason?" Sandra wondered.

"He said if I told him no, he could come back and ask Cicely for her number later." Toya laughed. "But if he tried to mack on me in front of y'all, and I curved him, he couldn't try to talk to you later, because you'd know he picked me first."

Normally Toya wouldn't admit that her boyfriend was once attracted to Cicely. But in her version of events Derrick picked her first, so it was okay. Sandra felt a little dejected, because Derrick hadn't mentioned her at all in that scenario.

"If Derrick told you that, why you tripping about that boy not coming up to us?" Sandra asked, in regards to the stranger in the mall.

"Because we're not at school, and I may never see that fool again," Toya explained. "When you're in a situation like that, you gotta man up and shoot your shot."

"Why don't you go talk to him then?" Sandra wondered.

"You think I won't?"

"No, I know you will."

"Bet," Toya said, still considering it a dare.

As she walked away, Sandra couldn't help but notice how awesome her friend's figure looked in those black stretch pants. Toya was fine enough to be in a music video. She had already taken some pictures with a wannabe photographer who said he was putting her portfolio together. That was six months ago. Sandra often wondered what became of those pics, but Toya was never interested enough to track the cameraman down.

"Why you hyping her up?" Cicely asked as Toya pursued the stranger down the escalators. She and Sandra followed at a distance.

"I didn't hyper her up. I was just wondering why she was complaining about something she could do herself."

"Have you ever done that?" Cicely asked her.

"Done what?"

"Went up to a boy and asked him for his number."

Sandra grinned and shook her head.

"Why not?"

She shrugged. "I don't know. I guess I'm too scary. My mama said I shouldn't do stuff like that, 'cause it'll make me look fast."

"You still not talking to anybody?"

Sandra shook her head. "Nope. Forever single."

"Not *forever*," Cicely said with a chuckle. "Just for now."

"When it comes to me, *for now* always lasts a long time," Sandra told her.

"Do you want me to try to hook you up with one of Byron's friends?"

"No. I don't like any of them."

"What about Reggie?"

"Umm, maybe."

Cicely noticed her fighting a smile. "Yeah, you like Reggie, don't you?"

"He's alright."

"He's cute," Cicely said. "And he doesn't smoke weed or get into any of the other bad stuff I know you don't wanna be around."

"I don't mind being around it," Sandra said. "I just don't wanna do it myself."

"You want me to give Reggie your number?"

"I don't know. I'll think about it," Sandra said.

By the time they got down the escalator, Toya was headed their way. She was typing something on her phone, so Sandra knew the expedition was a success.

"How'd it go?" Cicely asked.

"I got his number," Toya said. "I don't think I'm gonna call though."

"Why not?" Sandra wondered.

"He got a girlfriend," Toya explained. "He said I have to text him first, before I call. Ain't nobody got time for that."

"You had to text Roderick before you called him," Cicely recalled. "Didn't stop you then."

"That's because I already knew what Roderick was working with," Toya told them. "He was worth the trouble. But that fool," she said, shooting a thumb back at the guy she just met, "he has a fake watch on, and he's carrying a *Sears* bag. So I know he don't got no money. And his feet are little, so he probably got a *mini me!*"

● ● ● ● ● ●

After loitering in the mall for a couple of hours and not stealing anything – as far as Sandra could tell – the crew decided they were indeed ravenous. They stood in line at a Mexican eatery and ordered combos that came with three tacos and plenty of beans and rice.

Sandra was not surprised to see Toya pig out when they got their plates, but she was always taken aback by how much Cicely ate.

"How you stay so skinny?" she had to ask.

"I don't know," Cicely said. "My mama says it'll catch up with me sooner or later."

"Then you might finally grow some curves," Toya joked.

"I got curves," Cicely replied.

"You got boobs, but no junk in the trunk," Toya told her. "Sandra got more booty than you."

Cicely didn't argue that. Sandra was surprised by how good the comment made her feel.

Towards the end of their meal, Sandra got a call from her mother.

"Are you still at the mall?" Before she could respond, Dorothy said, "I'm on my way."

"Yes, we're still here."

"Meet me out front," her mother said. "Be out there waiting. I'm running late."

"Okay."

When she got off the phone, Sandra told her friends, "My mama's on her way to get me."

"Man, it's only six o'clock," Toya said, checking her phone.

"It's not like we're doing anything," Sandra stated.

"You gotta go home and watch the twins?" Cicely asked knowingly.

Sandra had three siblings in all. Her older brother Calvin was a sophomore at Texas Lutheran, the university Sandra had been accepted to. She couldn't wait to get there, so she could be at the same school as her brother again.

Her other siblings were Kim and Tim (technically Kimberly and Timothy). They were twins, in the seventh grade. Sandra had to look after them fairly often, but she never considered it a burden. The love she got from her family was one of the best feelings in the world.

"Yeah," she said as she gathered her food debris on a plastic tray.

"How long you got before she gets here?" Cicely asked.

"Probably about ten minutes. She wants me to be outside waiting."

"Your mama has a gun, so we'd better do what she says," Toya joked.

On the way to the front of the mall, the friends noticed another group of girls in the crowd.

Toya's eyes narrowed as she told her friends, "That's that ho Mary."

Sandra and Cicely followed her gaze. They saw three of their classmates walking together with the same nonchalance they exhibited. Personally Sandra didn't have a problem with any of them, but she knew Mary was Derrick's last girlfriend. For some reason, that put her and Toya at odds, even though Derrick never cheated on Mary.

"Forget them," Cicely said. "They ain't about nothing."

"Naw, Mary was talking noise at school," Toya said. "I bet she won't say nothing now that we're somewhere we can fight."

Hearing the word *fight* immediately increased Sandra's heart rate. Generally she was the most mild-mannered member of their group. But when it was time for war, she took on a new persona. As the hairs stood on her arms, she temporarily forgot that her mother was only minutes away.

Toya's heart began to speed up too as her nemesis grew nearer. She yelled, "What's up, ho?" which made everyone within a thirty feet radius turn to look at her.

By the time Mary realized she was the *ho* in question, Toya was within striking distance. Sandra and Cicely stood on either side of their friend, creating a unified front of meanness. Not to be outdone, Mary's friends stepped forward to back her up.

Mary was a big girl – not terribly overweight, but she had more fat stacked on her than Toya did. Mary also had an ugly, pink extension wrapped around her itty-bitty ponytail. If there was one thing Sandra knew about hoodrats, it was that any girl who had the nerve to throw a pink ponytail on

70

her head with no qualms about how unnatural it looked could probably care less about losing said ponytail in a cat fight.

Luckily the two girls Mary was with were both underclassmen, and they were skinny. So if all hell broke loose, Sandra gave the edge to her team.

Mary put a hand on her hip and cocked her head. She fixed an annoyed expression on Toya.

"I know you ain't talking to me."

"Yeah, I'm talking to you," Toya spat. "With yo *fat ass*. What's up with all that noise you was talking at school?"

"You know you ain't about that life," Mary deduced. "That's why you always starting mess when we around a bunch of people."

"We can go outside," Toya suggested.

"Yeah, like they don't have security driving around," Mary said sarcastically.

"Let's go down the street then," Toya said. "Why you making excuses? You too fat to walk that far?"

"Girl, *bye*. You just as big as me," Mary pointed out. "I didn't say nothing to you, Toya. You better gone, before I get–"

"Before you get what?" Sandra said, taking a step forward. "What you gon' do?"

Mary looked from Toya to her new antagonizer.

"I know you better get out my face."

"If you got a problem with her, you got a problem with me, too," Sandra said. She looked Toya's rival up and down, daring her to make a move.

Mary snorted. She looked around and saw that a group of people were gathering around them. Her fists balled instinctively. "This the last time I'm gon' tell you to get out my face," she snarled.

"Or *what*?" Sandra balled her fists and took another step in her direction. "Do something about it!"

Cicely wasn't surprised that Sandra wanted to take the lead on this. All of her friends brought something different to the table. Sandra relished her role as enforcer.

"Alright! Enough! *Break it up!*"

Sandra didn't notice a security guard headed their way until he was standing between the two groups.

"Either break it up, or get out the mall!" the man yelled. "Whoever throws a punch gets banned for a year!"

Fighting was never really on the agenda, so the girls backed away from each other without a word. They kept their scowls in place, though, even as they turned and walked in opposite directions. Sandra didn't let her guard down until her crew made it outside and were greeted by a police car idling in the fire lane.

● ● ● ● ● ●

"Dang, they called the law on us already?" Toya commented, her eyes locked on the black and white patrol car.

But Cicely knew better. She told Sandra, "Ain't that your mom?" and Sandra nodded, a deep chill enveloping her.

It suddenly occurred to her how close they had just come to disaster. Sandra never expected Mary to throw a punch, but if the mall security had escorted them out of the building, her mother would've seen it, and she would have been very upset about it.

72

"Y'all need a ride home?" Sandra asked her friends as she walked away from them. She didn't bother waiting, because she already knew what they would say.

"I'm not riding in the back of a police car," Toya said indignantly. "Never that."

"Me neither," Cicely tacked on.

Sandra had to fight to keep from smiling, because her mother often told her Toya would spend a lot of time in the back of a police car when she was older, if she didn't change her ways while she was still in high school.

"Alright, well I guess I'll see y'all Monday," Sandra told them.

"You not doing anything this weekend?" Cicely asked.

"Probably not," Sandra said as she opened the front door of the squad car. "I'll let you know if I do."

"You'll let them know if you do *what*?" her mother asked before she had time to settle into her seat.

Sandra smiled at her as she fastened her safety belt. Her mother was pretty, but not in a Cover Girl kind of way. Dorothy didn't wear any makeup to work, and she looked a little butch in her police uniform. But she had beautiful, brown eyes and rich dark skin, like her daughter. Her shoulder-length hair was pulled back in a ponytail. Her bulletproof vest made her boobs appear nonexistent, but they were under there, and most men thought they were perfect.

Sandra knew that her mother downplayed her looks while on the job, because "Perps might try to act crazy with a pretty, little thing." But there was nothing she could do to fully diminish her attractiveness. She was currently dating another officer on the force, but she hadn't introduced him to the family yet. Her late husband died five years ago.

Dorothy wasn't sure how Sandra and the twins would react when she told them she was ready to move on.

"They don't want a ride home?" she asked when Sandra closed her door.

"No. They don't wanna ride in the back," her daughter replied.

"You'll let them know if you do what?" Dorothy asked again as she pulled away from the curb. She looked past her daughter and waved at her two friends. Toya and Cicely smiled and waved back dutifully.

"They were asking if I was getting out this weekend," Sandra said.

"You can if you want to," her mother replied. "I'm off Saturday."

"I don't think they have anything to do," Sandra said. "Plus I don't have any more money. I might go to Cicely's house for a while."

"What happened to your allowance?"

"I spent the last of it just now. We ate some tacos."

"Do you need more money?"

Sandra shook her head. "No. I can make it till Monday."

"Every time you go to the mall with them, I'm worried you'll call me from some store's security room," Dorothy revealed.

"They haven't done anything like that in a while," Sandra said.

"Thieves usually don't stop that easily," her mother said. "Every day I get calls on the same people. Over and over."

"Yeah, but those are *crackheads*," Sandra said with a chuckle.

Dorothy grinned. "Yes, that's true. I'll tell you one thing: I'm glad neither one of them are going to Texas Lutheran with you in the fall."

Sandra was not happy about that, so she didn't respond.

"I know those are your best friends," her mom said. "But I been putting bracelets on bad people for a long time. Trust me; I know trouble when I see it."

"They're not bad people," Sandra argued. "Cicely's going to college. She got accepted to TCU."

"Did she get a full ride?" Dorothy already knew the answer to that.

"No, but I didn't either," Sandra said.

"You can keep defending them if you want to," her mom replied. "But you know I'm right. I bet you can't tell me Toya is doing good – in school or in life."

Sandra tried to think of something positive to say about her other friend. She came up short.

"It's okay," her mother said. "You know I'm not gonna ask you to stop hanging around them. You're old enough to choose your friends."

They were stopped at a red light. Dorothy reached and placed her hand on Sandra's. The girl looked her in the eyes and smiled affectionately. The dimples that appeared on Sandra's cheeks soothed her mom's heart.

CHAPTER EIGHT
BY INVITATION ONLY

On Monday, May 18th, all of the seniors at Finley High were excited about a big party planned for the following Saturday. None of Cicely's friends left campus for lunch that day, so they were seated together in the cafeteria when the host of the affair made his way to their table to offer them a formal invite.

William Prince wasn't one of the cool kids at school, but last April he experienced a life-changing event that increased his popularity exponentially.

His parents got a divorce.

While that didn't earn him immediate kudos from his peers, the aftermath of his parents' breakup certainly did. His father moved to Dallas, leaving the house and the couple's only child with his wife. Noticing her son was in a slump after the divorce, William's mother suggested he throw a party at their home.

"Invite all of your school friends," she suggested.

William didn't have many friends at the time, so he invited anyone who seemed remotely interested, and about thirty students showed up. No one knew what to expect, but the evening turned out to be legendary.

Prior to the party, few people at Finley High knew that William's parents were rich. They weren't millionaires, but they had a two-story, eight bedroom home with an impressive below-ground pool out back, which made everyone view William as wealthy from that point on.

The other thing that made his party so exceptional was his mom Chelsea. Possibly still reeling from the divorce herself – she went out of her way to make William's party as spectacular as possible. In addition to endless snacks and drinks, she had a gift bag for all of the kids to take home when the bash shut down at midnight.

If that wasn't awesome enough, William's mom was rumored to have a prescription pill problem. She was a little *too* happy the entire evening. At times her speech was slurred. Later, one of the jocks said he was pretty sure she was trying to lure him into her bedroom.

But Chelsea's questionable behavior didn't detract from William's big night. On the contrary, it added to the allure.

William hosted two more parties since then. Each one was bigger and wilder than the first. Cicely had already heard about what was sure to be his grandest celebration to date before he walked up to their lunch table with a stack of flyers in hand.

"Hey. Y'all having a good day?"

William was biracial, with a black father and white mother. His skin was very fair. He had a smattering of freckles on his cheeks. His hair was cinnamon colored, like Malcolm X's.

"Yes," Cicely and Sandra said in unison. Their smiles were big and friendly.

"I don't know if you heard or not–"

"Yes, we heard," Toya said, cutting him off. "Give us the invitations!"

William chuckled as he handed each girl a flyer.

"This is going to be the last party I throw before we graduate," he said as the ladies examined their invites. "There won't be too many underclassmen. This one is for the *seniors*. I know a lot of students will be with their families on graduation night, so this may be the last chance we have to come together, before life takes us in different directions.

"Y'all should come. You know I have a pool, so you can bring your bathing suits. Your *bikinis*," he said with a grin that was slightly perverted. "It's supposed to be 93 degrees that day. But if it's not that hot, that's okay, because the pool is heated."

Cicely was nearly salivating as she listened to him. One last celebration with the Finley High class of 2015 sounded awesome. And it was a pool party! She definitely had the body for a two-piece swimsuit. She imagined herself strolling through William's home with no shirt on, just her bikini top. She'd have her booty shorts unbuttoned and unzipped, revealing her flat, sexy stomach, her cute belly button and a glimpse of the bottom half of her bathing suit.

"We'll be there," she told William. "I already can't wait."

"Me, neither," Toya told him. "You be doing it big, big Willie."

He grinned anxiously. It was clear he still wasn't used to his newfound fame.

"The only thing is," he said, "I don't want y'all to invite anyone. *I'll* invite everyone I want to come. Last time things got a little out of hand. Someone snuck up to my mom's room and stole some of her jewelry."

"What?" Toya's eyes were wide and disbelieving, although she heard about the theft already and could even give him the name of the culprit. "For real?"

"Yeah," William said. "That was messed up. My mom does a lot for us. She doesn't have to let me have parties at the house. She pays for everything; all the food, drinks..."

"That's wrong," Cicely said. "It was probably some straight up *hoodrats*."

"Yeah," he agreed. "But anyway, I wanna make sure nothing bad happens this time, so please don't invite anyone. If there's somebody you want me to invite, tell me and let me do it. I know it sounds mean, but there's some people at this school who can't come to my party. And I don't want anybody from other schools, either. I don't want people bringing their cousins or their homegirl from down the street..."

The girls laughed, though it was clear he was serious.

"Don't worry," Cicely told him. "We won't invite anybody. We're happy you like us enough to let us come."

"Oh, you girls are great," William said. "I'll, um, I'll see you around."

He walked away in search of the next lucky student who would be allowed to attend his big shindig.

"Ooh, girl, this party is gon' be so *crunk*!" Toya exclaimed.

"I know," Cicely agreed. "I was already thinking about what bathing suit I'm gonna wear."

"I know you gon' wear a two-piece," Toya said.

"Already!"

"I'ma get faded that night," Toya told them.

"I'll bring some blunts," Cicely offered.

"He'll let y'all get high at the party?" Sandra asked.

"No, but his mom gets so wasted, she can't hardly tell what's going on," Toya explained. "Last time William had a party, somebody put gin in all of the punch bowls. Even people who didn't wanna drink got messed up!"

Cicely found that hilarious. Sandra didn't know what to think.

"Are you gonna smoke with us at the party?" Toya asked her.

Sandra shrugged. "I don't know."

"You should," Cicely said. "It's our last party before graduation. You gotta do the *most* that night. Trust me, you'll have *waaay* more fun."

"Alright," Sandra said with a giggle.

"Do you think you can get your mom's car on Saturday?" Toya asked Cicely.

Sandra had her driver's license too, but her mother was a lot stricter when it came to handing over her car keys. If Sandra mentioned that Cicely and Toya would be involved, that was almost guaranteed to get her shut down every time.

"I might be able to get it," Cicely said.

"If not, how we gon' get there?" Toya wondered.

"Don't worry," Cicely told her. "Where there's a will, there's a way. This is gonna be the biggest party of the year. If worst comes to worst, I'll get my cousin Peabody to take us."

"Bet," Toya said. "Now the only thing I'm worried about is too many lames."

"What you mean?" Sandra asked.

"If William's only inviting who *he* wants, he probably ain't inviting any cool people."

"He invited us," Sandra pointed out.

"Yeah, but that's because we're girls, and we're fine," Toya explained. "Every party got to have some fine girls. I'm talking about the *boys*. I bet he's only inviting squares."

"Man, if we go, and it's nothing but lames there, I'ma be pissed," Cicely said.

"Then we gotta make sure that doesn't happen," Toya said with one of her sinister smiles.

● ● ● ● ● ●

When the girls left the cafeteria, they ran into Toya's *would-be* boyfriend Derrick and a couple of his friends chilling near the portable buildings. The boys weren't doing anything bad at the time, but they had an aura about them that made people wary.

Sandra felt self-conscious the moment she and Chris locked eyes. She'd only seen him in passing a few times since their ill-fated hook-up on Derrick's filthy couch last Friday. On those occasions, Sandra had averted her attention and kept walking. But there was nowhere to run to this time.

Chris surprised her by saying, "Hey, what's up, Sandra?"

Her eyes widened. She didn't think he remembered her name.

"You thought I forgot your name, didn't you?" he said with a smirk.

Today he wore skinny jeans with black Chuck's and a black tee shirt. Sandra thought he was super fine. The bad things she recently learned about him pushed his sexiness up another notch.

"When are we gonna kick it again?" he asked her. "You need to give me your number."

Sandra was stunned speechless. Never – not once – had she been the first one a guy talked to when she was with her friends. Her heart danced as she removed her cellphone from her pocket and unlocked it for him.

"Here. You can, you can put your number in my phone," she told Chris as she handed it over.

"What y'all finna do?" Derrick asked Toya. He stepped to her and wrapped both arms around her, bringing her in for a hug.

Toya pushed him away when his hands started to descend towards her backside.

"Boy, stop."

"What's wrong?" he asked. "Why you tripping?"

"You know Mr. Walters don't play that," she said, referring to the school's tougher-than-nails principal.

Mr. Walters was known to patrol the school during lunchtime. If he caught Derrick with his hands on Toya's rump, they'd both get detention.

"What's that?" Chris asked Sandra after he returned her phone.

"Oh, it's an invitation," she told him. "William's having a party this Saturday."

"*Ooh, y'all gotta go!*" Toya exclaimed. She gave her flyer to Derrick. "It's gonna be off the chain! His parties are always epic. We're gonna get faded."

"Why he didn't give me a flyer?" Derrick wanted to know. "I just saw that punk in third period. I saw him handing these out..."

"I don't know," Toya said. "But he said we can invite other people, if we wanted to."

"Man, I ain't trying to go to that fool's party," Derrick said as he studied the invite.

"Why not?" Toya asked. "It's gonna be a pool party. Don't tell me you don't wanna see us in our bikinis..."

Derrick looked her up and down and his expression softened. "Shoo, who wouldn't wanna see that?"

"Exactly," Toya said.

"You gonna be there, too?" his friend Kevin asked Cicely.

Kevin played on the basketball team with the other two, but his lackluster grades kept him off the court most of the time. He took the label "dumb jock" a little too seriously. But, as far as the girls were concerned, his looks made up for his poor reading skills. Out of all of the cute players on the team, Kevin was in the top three.

"I'll be there," Cicely told him.

"Dang, you fine," Kevin said, sizing her up. "You should give me your number, in case I wanna see you *before* the party."

Cicely chuckled. Her smile was agreeable, but her mouth said, "Can't do that. I got a boyfriend."

"I figured that," Kevin said, "as fine as you are. But where he at tho'?"

"He had to make up a test for Mr. Bowden," Cicely said, grinning flirtatiously.

"You never cheat on him?" Kevin asked. "You get high?"

She shook her head. "No, I haven't cheated on him – *yet*. And yeah, I smoke."

83

Sandra was surprised by the way her friend was responding to him. She shook her head, giggling.

Either Kevin didn't know the rules of engagement when it came to a group of girls, or he didn't give a damn, because he quickly moved his attention from Cicely to Toya.

"What about you, shorty? You got a man?"

Sandra thought either Derrick or Toya would be offended by that, but her friend continued to smile.

"Yeah, I'm working on this one right here," Toya said and pushed Derrick playfully on the chest.

He caught her hand and pulled her in for another hug. This time he wrapped his arms around her midsection so Toya couldn't get away.

"Check out that bubble!" he told his friend.

Kevin stepped forward to admire Toya's rump while she struggled with Derrick.

"It is nice," Kevin noticed.

"Grab it," Derrick told him. "You gotta feel how soft it is."

"You bet not!" Toya squealed.

She continued to struggle, but Derrick only outweighed her by ten pounds. Sandra knew that if Toya really wanted to get out of his grip, she could have.

Rather than squeeze her butt, Kevin gave it a playful slap.

"*Stop, boy*! Don't be touching me!" Toya screamed, and she began to fight a little harder.

Derrick let go of her, and he and his friends laughed jovially.

"You a *buster*!" Toya yelled at Derrick. She tried to look angry, but being the object of so much desire was thrilling for her. She couldn't stop a smile from creeping to the corner of her mouth.

"Hey, it ain't no fun, if the homies can't have none!" Derrick said.

His friends readily agreed.

"I can't stand you!" Toya told him. She turned and walked away. Her friends did the same.

"What the hell was that?" Cicely asked when they rounded the corner and were no longer within sight of the boys.

"Nothing," Toya said. Her confident smile was back in place. "They was just playing."

"That didn't look like a game to me," Cicely told her. "He let Kevin touch all on you. He *told* him to do it."

"Derrick's stupid," Toya told her. "And he's not my man. If he was my man, it would be different."

She dropped the conversation, as if her explanation was sufficient.

Before Cicely could ask about Derrick's "*it ain't no fun, if the homies can't have none*" comment, the lunch bell rang. The girls were engulfed in organized chaos as students hurried to make it to their lockers before their next class.

Cicely didn't have fourth period with either of her friends. She told them she'd catch them later before heading upstairs. On the way to her algebra class, she ran into Serena and Jamar, who were exiting Mrs. Harding's classroom.

Cicely felt a little guilty when she saw them, because she knew they had just left a meeting for Jamar's bible club. Cicely used to go to those meetings herself, but there were too many distractions for her at lunchtime. Plus she had yet to repent or turn away from her sins, so why bother pretending to be something she wasn't?

She gave Serena a hug in the middle of the hallway.

"Hey, girl! What you been up to?"

"Nothing much," Serena said. She and Cicely continued to hold hands when they separated.

"Hey, Jamar," Cicely said.

"Hi," he said. "Good to see you, Cicely. Wish you would come to more of our meetings. We really miss you..."

Cicely smiled, but she didn't respond to that. "So, what's up with y'all?" she asked them. "Y'all going out now, or what?"

"We're just friends," Serena said right away.

Cicely gave her a look that said she didn't believe that. "Yeah, *okay*... Are y'all coming to William's party this Saturday?"

Serena shook her head while Jamar raised an eyebrow.

"That's the one we were talking about," she told him. "Remember that flyer I showed you?"

"Oh, William Prince," Jamar said.

"Why aren't you going?" Cicely asked her friend.

"Jamar doesn't like parties like that," Serena stated. "You know William's mom gets drunk every time. After that, anything goes. They were smoking weed out by the pool last time. People were stealing stuff out of his house..." She shook her head.

Cicely was blown away by Serena's new outlook. Before she got pregnant, parties like that were right up her alley. Cicely was also taken aback by the way Serena mentioned Jamar's likes and dislikes ahead of her own. She sounded like they had been together for years.

"Why y'all playing?" she asked them. "Why don't y'all hurry up and get married already?"

Jamar's eyes widened. His cheeks reddened with embarrassment.

Cicely walked away chuckling before Serena could lash out at her.

CHAPTER NINE
GIRL ON FIRE

Do I know what love really is?
Or am I just blinded by it?
Will I ever truly understand?
Or should I be slammed
Or maybe even crammed
In the search for love?
Love is a prison, I think...

Sandra had to head straight home after school because her mother worked from five to one a.m. Sandra had to be there to look after the twelve year old twins. Her older brother Calvin moved out of the house already. Sandra missed him terribly and was glad he was never too far away. Between his gun fanaticism and her mother's career as a police officer, Sandra always felt safe and protected.

The only thing missing from the picture was her dad, who died when the twins were seven. He got the big C, and everyone watched him grow sicker and sicker. He was surrounded by his loving family when he took his last breath. Sandra sometimes wondered if she was luckier or if the twins had it better. They were so young when he passed away, she doubted if their memories were very vivid. Sandra, on the other hand, had plenty of time to get to know her dad and adore him. She kept her favorite picture of him on her bedroom dresser.

By seven p.m. that night she had the twins fed. They said they didn't have any homework, so she made them read for an hour. She did not let them turn on the Xbox, because their mother determined that would only be a weekend or summertime activity. But she did go against the grain and let them watch a few episodes of South Park.

With the twins glued to the television and no homework of her own to do, Sandra's night started to drag. She called her friend Cicely but got no help there.

"I'm on the phone with Byron."

"Can't you call him back?"

"I can call *you* back."

"You shouldn't put a boy before your homegirl," Sandra told her.

"I would never do that," Cicely assured her. "Bye!"

Sandra struck out with Toya as well.

"I'm on the phone."

"With who, Derrick?"

"No. Kevin?"

"Kevin? The one who smacked you on the booty today?"

"Yeah."

"Wha, how did that happen?"

"I was on the phone with Derrick, and he pissed me off, so I told him to give me Kevin's number. He did, and now I'm on the phone with Kevin."

"But, but they're like best friends."

"No. I don't think so."

"I knew you liked the way they were playing with you. I don't know why you were trying to fight."

"Okay. Bye," Toya said.

"Wait. I'm bored."

"Didn't Chris give you his number today?"

"Yeah."

"Why don't you call him?"

"I'm scared," Sandra admitted.

"I know you are. But which would you rather be, scared or bored and lonely? Bye," Toya said, and she disconnected.

Sandra sighed. She searched the contacts on her phone and found Chris' number. She actually felt better about calling him *before* she talked to Toya. Now she understood that Derrick and his friends flipped girls like coins. They never stayed with anyone long enough to care for them or fall in love.

But did she really need love? Yes, in the long run she surely did. But she didn't have to think about the long run with every boy she talked to. Even her mother told her that.

She pressed the "Call" button under Chris' name before she chickened out.

After four rings, Sandra thought the call was going to voicemail, but a strong voice came to the line and asked, "Who's this?"

Sandra didn't realize she was holding her breath until she found herself unable to speak.

After a couple of seconds, Chris sounded annoyed when he said, "Yo, who is this?"

"Sorry," Sandra gasped. She felt perspiration on her face and underarms. "It's me, Sandra. You, you gave me your number today..."

He chuckled. Sandra assumed he was laughing at her. She felt even more self-conscious. This was a terrible idea. She wondered how awkward things would be at school tomorrow if she hung up now.

"I know who you are," he said. "Why you keep thinking I'm gonna forget you?"

Sandra had a lot of answers to that question. She chose to keep them to herself.

"I don't know. I, you didn't seem like you liked me, the last time I saw you."

"When? Today?"

"No. I mean last week. Friday, at Derrick's."

"My bad," he said. "I wasn't feeling it that day. I didn't want to be at Derrick's nasty house in the first place. I didn't mean to diss you or nothing."

"You didn't diss me," Sandra said, though she felt that was exactly what had happened. Chris kissed her, and then walked out on her when she wouldn't smoke his weed or let him touch between her legs. That rejection was as blatant as it could be.

"I'm sorry for disrespecting you like that," he said.

Sandra was so taken aback, she found herself frowning as she sat up in her bed. Her heart was going a mile a minute.

"Sometimes Derrick introduces me to girls," Chris went on, "and they don't even want to know my name. I try to get to know them, but they just wanna... You know. But you different. You not like that, and that's what I like about you. You special."

91

Sandra's eyes were wide and disbelieving. But her heart wanted to believe anyway. It began to beat slow and steady now. Her whole body was enveloped in a warm, radiating heat.

"And I know everybody doesn't smoke weed," Chris continued. "I shouldn't have tried to pass that to you. You probably think I'm a thug now, huh, because I smoke?"

"No," Sandra said. "I don't think that."

"You ever smoked before?"

She shook her head as she said, "No."

"Not even cigarettes?"

"Nope."

"You don't drink either, then, right?"

"I have, a couple of times."

"You got drunk?"

"No. It was just a couple of sips."

"Dang. You a good girl for real."

Sandra smiled. The same characteristics that made most of her peers consider her "lame" seemed to have a different effect on Chris.

"What did you think about me smoking?" he asked. "You don't think I'm a bad person?"

"Oh, no," Sandra said. She couldn't believe he cared about what she thought of him. Did that mean he really liked her? She didn't want to get her hopes up, but all signs were pointing in that direction.

"Then what do you think?" he asked.

"To each his own," she replied. "It's not hurting me."

"I won't do it around you, if you don't like it," he said. "I'm trying to quit anyway."

"It would be better if you quit," Sandra said, hoping she wasn't overstepping. "It's not good for you, especially if you smoke cigarettes, too."

"I don't smoke cigarettes," he said. "I wouldn't be able to run track if I did."

"The weed doesn't keep you from running?" Sandra was genuinely curious about that.

"No, but I think it will after a while."

"How long you been smoking?"

"I just started this year."

"What's it like?" she asked.

"What, getting high?"

"Yeah."

After a pause, he said, "Why?"

"I don't know. I always ask people."

"You sound like you wanna smoke. That's how it started with me: First I wanted to know what it was like, and then I had to find out for myself."

"I do think about it," Sandra acknowledged.

"Okay, now you got me confused," he said with a chuckle. "I thought you was supposed to help me get off weed. How you gon' do that, if you smoking too?"

"You want me to help you get off weed?" Sandra was thrilled.

"I think it would be cool to be with somebody who wants to help me," Chris said, "instead of somebody who only wants to get turnt-up every chance they get."

For Sandra, this conversation felt like a big roller coaster ride, except there were no descents. It was steadily going up and up. She heard everything Chris said, but her mind was stuck on the words "*would be cool to be with somebody....*" Did he really like her like that?

The fear that kept her safely tucked inside her own personal cocoon on most days warned her to take it easy. But it was that same fear that kept her so far down on Finley High's social ladder, compared to her best friends.

"If you *do* decide you want to get high," Chris said, "you should only do it once or twice a month. Not every day. Maybe if you're at a party or something."

"That would be cool," Sandra said. She lay back on her bed and settled in for what she hoped would be a long, flirtatious conversation.

● ● ● ● ● ●

By nine o'clock the twins had bathed and were almost ready for bed. Sandra plopped down on the living room sofa with her lifeline to the world (aka cellphone) in hand. She noticed that she had a new friend request on Facebook. It was from a classmate named Peter Scott.

She accepted the request and then went to check out Peter's Facebook profile. Nothing special there, which was what she expected because Peter wasn't anything special either. He was an attractive-enough guy, but in all four years of high school, he never created any splashes or even an impressive ripple of waves on the social scene. Sandra thought she'd heard that he was an occasional target of bullies.

After checking out some of his profile pictures, she decided Peter was a lot cuter than she'd given him credit for. He had toffee brown skin, slightly curly hair, no braces or glasses. Sandra didn't spot any obvious reasons for Peter's supposed bullying, but that didn't mean anything. Some people don't need a reason to make your life a living hell. *Just because* will suffice.

Sandra was about to take a shower and get ready for bed when she received another notification from Facebook. This time she had a personal message. It was from Peter Scott, of all people.

The message simply read, "Hey, Sandra"

She considered not responding at all, but that would be rude. Peter was in her 4th period history class. She didn't want him to act funny around her tomorrow.

She wrote back, "Hey"

She waited, and sure enough a few dots appeared in her message box; indicating Peter was typing again.

I just found you on facebook

Sandra didn't know if that warranted a response, so she didn't type anything.

Do you think I could have your number?" Peter asked. "I want to call you."

Sandra was surprised to find herself at odds with the request. She didn't consider herself to be one of the coolest kids at school. But Toya and Cicely were, which made her cool by association. If she and Chris started going out, which seemed like an unbelievably real possibility, she would rise even higher on the popularity scale.

But talking to Peter wouldn't help at all. As a matter of fact, her swag would take a hit if she started palling around with a loser like him.

She caught herself. Did she want to start being superficial, like Toya? Just because Chris was seemingly interested in her didn't mean she was *all that* all of a sudden. She felt ashamed of herself for having this mental conversation. She gave Peter her number and then went to her bedroom.

He called before she could get in the tub.

"Hello?"

"Hi. This is Peter, from school."

"Hey." Sandra sat on the corner of her bed, not sure what to expect.

"Did you, um, are you busy?"

"No, not really," she said. "About to get in the shower."

"Oh, I can let you go, if you want."

She did want that, but she also wanted to know why he called.

"I got a minute. What's up?"

"Oh, uh, did, did you finish Mr. Forsythe's homework?"

Sandra's eyes flashed open. "Oh my God! No, I forgot."

"It's not that hard," Peter said. "I just finished it. I can help you with it, if you want..."

She checked the clock. At this point she needed a lot more than help with the assignment. She needed Peter to give her all of the answers.

"Okay," she said, scrambling now. "Let me get my notebook."

"That's, um, that's not the only reason I called," he said as she rummaged through her backpack.

"Oh. Well, what's up?" she asked.

"I was wondering if you wanted to go out sometimes."

She could tell that it was hard for him to ask her that. And she was flattered, despite the fact that Peter wasn't well-respected at school.

"I'll still help you with your homework, even if you say no," he added. "I think you're really nice. It's cool, if you only want to be friends."

She smiled. His sensitivity and low expectations reminded her of herself. She told him, "I didn't say I didn't want to go out with you."

"Oh. Okay. I guess I'll keep my hopes up, for now..."

"Okay," she said. She was all smiles as she found the history work in her backpack.

● ● ● ● ● ●

Before Sandra went to bed at 11:30, her friend Cicely finally dialed her number.

"Girl, what took you so long to call back?"

"I'm sorry," Cicely said. "I just got home."

"Where you been?"

"I had to help my sister with some stuff. It's been crazy in my neighborhood. We had two fights around the corner."

"Two fights? You weren't in them, were you?"

"No," Cicely said. "We were too high to fight." She laughed. "I recorded one of them on my phone. I'll show it to you tomorrow."

"Okay," Sandra said. "Girl, guess what..."

"What?"

"*I'm on fire*," she gushed. "It's raining men over here!"

"Really? Who?"

"I called Chris. He said he likes me. He wants to go out."

"For real?"

"Yeah." Sandra felt jittery all over again. "He said he wanted to stop smoking, and I could probably help him. He's way different than he was when we went to Derrick's house."

"I don't know about that one," Cicely said.

Sandra felt her heart sink. Why was there always someone there to crush her spirits?

"Why you say that?" she asked.

"You saw the way Derrick and his friends were," Cicely reminded her. "First Kevin tried to holler at me, and then he went right after Toya. Smacked her on the booty. They think we're all freaks."

"But, but Chris wasn't coming at me like that," Sandra said. "He was happy that I don't drink or smoke."

"Really?" Cicely said. "You believe that? Don't let him run game on you. I think he'll say whatever he can to get your panties off. First he tried to jump right in, right, but you stopped him. Then he tried to get you high, but that didn't work either. Now he's saying he likes you because you don't smoke..."

Sandra was crushed. Of course that's why Chris said all of those nice things. He just wanted to get laid, and then he'd be gone with the wind. But there was a chance Cicely was wrong about him. Sandra wanted to give him the benefit of the doubt, though common sense was on Cicely's side.

"But anyway," Cicely said, "who else did you talk to? You said it's raining men over there..."

Now Sandra didn't want to say. "Peter Scott," she revealed with a sigh.

After a pause, Cicely said, "Peter has your number?"

"I gave it to him today. He sent me a message on Facebook."

"That's cool," Cicely said. "Peter's a... He's, he's a good dude."

Sandra lowered her head in defeat. Her friend sounded like she was trying to find something nice to say about an ugly baby.

"Alright. I gotta go," she said.

"Wait. Are you mad?" Cicely asked. "I'm not trying to say Chris doesn't like you. I was just warning you that he *might be* running game."

"No, it's fine."

"And Peter is a really nice person," Cicely stressed. But that didn't help much. Cicely never described a boy as "really nice" unless she also thought he was ugly.

"I'm not tripping," Sandra said.

"Alright. But I do think Peter would be better for you," Cicely told her. "I know it's cool when the popular boys flirt with you, but Derrick and his friends do too much. If you do talk to Chris, you'll have to keep your guard up all the time."

"Alright," Sandra said. "I'll see you tomorrow at school."

"Okay. You sure you're not mad at me? Don't be mad."

"I'm not mad. Just sleepy."

"Okay. I'll see you tomorrow."

"Alright. Bye."

CHAPTER TEN
ALMA

This is going to be a lonely long life
This monster I call love gives me a fright
I always feel it
It makes me do stupid things
Like trip over my shoes
And wish I had wings...

The next morning Cicely was on her cellphone less than a minute after opening her eyes. She slept with it beneath her pillow. The date was Wednesday, May 20th, nine days till graduation.

Cicely was lucky to have a bedroom all to herself. She had plenty of privacy. Her mom even closed the door for her after the wakeup call, even though there were no boys in the house other than her dad. Cicely was grateful to have two parents who were still together. They were both hard-working. But they often said their lives would be better if they continued their education past high school. They always stressed that: Going to college is important.

As she wiped the sleep from her eyes, Cicely saw that she had a new friend request on Facebook. It was from a classmate named Alma Fuentes. Cicely wasn't friends with the girl in real life, but she didn't mind accepting her request in the virtual world. She then checked out a few pictures Alma had posted on the site. A lot of them made her raise an eyebrow. Alma seemed pretty basic at school, but on Facebook she was doing the most. She had plenty of shots showing off her cleavage, her puckered lips and her measly cakes.

Cicely checked out a few more notifications and then moved on to Instagram and Twitter. Six minutes after she turned her phone on, she was finally ready to get out of bed.

She took a shower and dressed in skinny jeans with a little tee-shirt. Cicely was the tallest and thinnest girl in her crew. She was never jealous of Toya, who probably had the best figure, because Cicely believed she was the prettiest.

When she got back to her phone, she had another notification from Alma on Facebook. It was a direct message:

Leave my man alone

Cicely blinked ten times in two seconds as she stared at the message. Tilting her head to the side did not help her decipher the words on her phone screen. Cicely's heart began to squeeze uncomfortably. Her bedroom darkened as a sudden gloom cloud blocked out the light from her ceiling fan.

Okay, this was confusing, but there were facts here as well. First of all, Alma had purposely befriended her on Facebook to deliver this cryptic message. Second, Alma knew that they would be face to face at school in less than an hour. Cicely wondered if she was afraid of a confrontation, or if she was trying to initiate one. But the third and foremost fact was that Alma was wrong. Cicely was going with Byron, and Byron was most certainly not going with Alma.

The mere thought of it made her cringe.

Ewww.

Cicely attempted to remain calm as she typed:

What the hell you talking about?

She stared fiercely at the screen, willing Alma to reply. She checked the time of the initial message. It was sent four minutes ago, while Cicely was styling her hair. She wondered if Alma had been waiting for her to respond. She got an answer to that and her other question in less than thirty seconds.

Byron

Cicely's heart dropped *way* down, all the way to her feet. Her legs were weak. She sat on the bed, her eyes glued to the phone. Her mind raced. Images of Byron bombarded her psyche. They were mashed up with the slutty pictures Alma posted on Facebook. Cicely thought of the way Alma looked at school, where her locker was, whether she had ever seen her and Byron talking or walking together.

Overall Cicely couldn't believe Byron was cheating on her – not with this *nobody*. But her body reacted like she believed it. She couldn't help it. Her heart shot back up to her chest and began to knock hard, uncomfortably so. Her breaths were hot and moist. There was fire in her eyes, but there were tears there, too. She fought to keep them from falling. This liar wasn't worth it.

You're clearly confused, she wrote. Unless you're talking about a different Byron.

There. She was proud of herself. She had remained calm, online at least.

But Alma replied, Byron Cooper, and all of Cicely's calm vacated the premises.

Her breaths were audible as she typed, You lying

Alma quickly responded. No I'm not

You're not with Byron, Cicely insisted. She stared at her phone as if the secret of life might be found within. Her knee bounced anxiously.

Alma's next response took forever. Cicely expected a whole paragraph, but her classmate simply wrote, He cheated on you. Been cheating. I know I'm wrong, but he want to be with me now

Cicely's eyes were wide and unblinking as she read the message again and again. There was no way! But then again, what would Alma stand to gain from this lie? She was going to get popped in the mouth – that fist was coming regardless. But why would Alma want that, if she wasn't really messing around with Byron? Most girls would avoid a fat lip, unless the prize was worth it.

Someone knocked on Cicely's door. She looked up with a fierce expression when the visitor entered without waiting for a response. It was her little sister Tanya. Of course it was. She was the only person in the house who would invade Cicely's personal space like that.

"Dang, what's wrong with you?" Tanya asked, noticing her demeanor.

Tanya started the school year as a sophomore at Finley High. But she had recently been transferred to Piedmont; an alternative school that struggled to educate kids with all sorts of bad behavior. Since kindergarten, Tanya had been in trouble for everything from biting to stealing. She was currently on Piedmont's roster for viciously assaulting a classmate. She couldn't wait to get back to Finley High next year, even though her dear sister would be gone to college by then.

"This ho starting some mess," Cicely growled. "Talking about she's messing with Byron."

Tanya came and sat next to her on the bed. Cicely showed her the conversation she and Alma were having on Facebook. Tanya had the phone in her hand when Alma responded again.

"She sent a picture."

"What?" Cicely couldn't imagine why.

"It's Byron," Tanya said.

Cicely took the phone and suffered a second heartbreak when she saw that Alma had indeed sent a picture of Byron in their conversation thread. It was a photo Cicely had never seen before. That made sense because it had obviously been taken with Alma's phone.

Before the tears welled in her eyes, Cicely recognized the shirt Byron was wearing. It was a collar shirt; a Polo with blue and white stripes. It was one of his favorites. He wore it infrequently enough to make it look special each time.

Cicely also thought Byron looked uncomfortable in the picture, like she'd popped up on him paparazzi style. Or maybe that was a guilty look in his eyes, because he knew the picture could be used as evidence of his infidelities. The more she stared at his expression, the more Cicely knew that was surely the answer.

She also determined that she didn't recognize the background in the photo. Byron was outside somewhere other than school. Was it Alma's house? Cicely refused to believe he would do that to her. What the hell did Alma have that she didn't? Not one thing!

She started to type a response, but Cicely backed out of Facebook instead. Why argue with this liar when she could go directly to the source? Byron was at the top of the "Favorites" list in her contacts. She called him and stared anxiously into her little sister's eyes as the phone rang.

"Hey, what's up?" Byron said. He sounded completely normal. Apparently Alma hadn't told him about her plans this morning.

Cicely cut straight to the chase. "Do you know Alma?"

He took too long to answer. Cicely's hand trembled. She pushed the phone closer to her face to keep her sister from noticing. She swallowed hard and felt her heart breaking for a third time. Soon there would be nothing left but a pile of lumpy, pulsating flesh in her chest.

"The one who goes to school with us?" he asked.

She blew steam from her nostrils. "Yeah."

She felt like her voice was shaky, but it didn't sound like it was. She looked up at Tanya, who was subconsciously looking to her big sister for guidance. Regardless of how dreadful she felt, Cicely knew that she had to keep it together. She had to lead by example.

"She's in my P.E. class," Byron said. "Why? What about her?"

"What about her? Why don't you tell me?"

Unfortunately Cicely had been cheated on before. She prayed she wasn't experiencing that again, because she really did love Byron. Her mother doubted that she truly understood her feelings. But Cicely was eighteen, which was old enough to know if she was in love.

"Bae, why don't you just say what you got to say? I didn't do nothing. I don't know what's going on."

His term of endearment and his denial caused a soothing coolness to envelope her. But Cicely kept her features hard and rigid.

"She sent me a message on Facebook," she told him. "She said y'all together now, and I need to leave you alone."

There was another noticeable pause. It would've been nice if Byron said, "*What*?" or "*Aw, hell naw!*" immediately, but he didn't. Instead he paused. Was he thinking of another lie? Was he shocked silent because Alma told him she'd keep their affair a secret?

The longer it took for him to respond, the more Cicely began to accept that it was all true. It was a devastating blow. She thought they had a future. When she got to college, she planned to get a job, and so did he. They had talked about getting an apartment together.

"Baby, she's lying," he said.

"Why it take you so long to answer?" she breathed.

"Because I'm sitting here tripping, wondering what the hell is going on."

"You never talked to her?"

"I talk to her at school sometimes, but–"

"You ever talk to her outside of school? You ever *see* her outside of school?"

And there was the pause again. Cicely shook her head at her sister, indicating she wouldn't believe anything he said from this point on. Tanya shook her head in dismay as well. All boys were dogs. No matter how good they seemed in the beginning, they would eventually get bored and go on the prowl.

"I saw her yesterday," Byron said.

Cicely was surprised to hear that. She believed it was probably true, but there were plenty more lies to come. She just had to be smart enough to know the difference.

"When I was walking my dog," he continued, "she was at the park with her brother and sisters. I stopped and talked to her for a minute, but that was it. She said she liked me, and I told her I was with you."

Cicely's eyes narrowed, and a few of the burning tears spilled. She hated herself for it. She also hated herself for wanting to believe his story. It did sound a little plausible. If Alma was as dumb as she looked, she might be trying to drive a wedge between the happy couple, hoping she could have Byron if Cicely broke up with him. It was a childish ploy, but whores don't reason like regular people.

"Alright then, we'll both go talk to her today, when we get to school," Cicely decided. She sounded strong and sure of herself. She didn't feel it, but she wiped her tears and convinced herself that she could handle this, no matter how it turned out.

"Okay," Byron said. "That's cool. I can't even believe she did that. I told her I didn't wanna be with her."

Cicely had a million other questions, like how a random conversation turned into Alma saying she wanted to be with him and how Alma managed to take his picture. She decided to save those questions until they were all face to face. She didn't need to catch Byron in a multitude of lies. She only needed to catch him in *one*. No matter how much she loved him, she wouldn't let him play her for a fool.

As for Alma, Cicely couldn't wait to tell her friends. The girl was stupid on top of ugly, if she thought she could pull this mess without getting her head knocked in.

"Alright, we'll find out when we get to school," she told Byron.

"Okay, baby, but—"

She hung up on him.

"He said he didn't do it?" Tanya asked.

Cicely nodded as she pulled up Facebook on her phone again. "Yeah, but we'll find out who's lying when we get to school. That girl didn't inbox me for nothing."

"What are you doing now?" Tanya asked. She watched her sister type a quick message.

"I told her we'll settle it when we get to school."

Cicely started to call Toya, but she checked the time and saw that she was already running late. She only had ten minutes left for breakfast. She stood and stuffed her phone in her back pocket.

Tanya stood too. "Are you gonna call Toya and them?" she asked.

"Yeah, but not right now. I don't want Mama to hear me."

"I wish I was back at Finley," Tanya said. "We could whoop that girl all up and down the hall. Snatch her hair out. I swear I'd beat the shi—"

"*Tanya!*"

The girls turned and saw their mother standing in the doorway. She fixed hard, fed-up eyes on Tanya, who could never seem to do right.

Tanya looked from her to Cicely, her eyes wide and disbelieving.

If it wasn't such a tense moment, Cicely would've laughed at her. Time and time again Tanya got busted for everything she did. Sometimes she even got in trouble for Cicely's transgressions.

"Who you talking about fighting?" their mother demanded to know. "You already got kicked out of school, Tanya! That's not enough for you? You haven't learned your lesson yet?!"

Nancy was a strong woman, short and stout. Cicely knew she got her looks and her height from her dad, who teetered over six feet, three inches tall.

Despite her flaws, Tanya was always loyal. She grumbled, "I'm not fighting nobody," under her breath, rather than snitch on Cicely.

Nancy stood in the doorway with both hands on her hips. She shook her head slowly. Her look of disappointment was so familiar, Tanya could see it with her eyes closed.

Their mother worked as a receptionist at an attorney's office. It was her legal contacts that helped Cicely out of a bind a couple of years ago when she and Toya got caught stealing from JC Penney's. Since then Cicely had been on the straight and narrow, as far as Nancy knew. She had a few blemishes on her report card every now and then, but for the most part she put forth an effort to make her mama proud.

"What's going on now?"

That booming voice came from their father. Cicely heard him approaching from the master bedroom.

"Tanya's in here talking about fighting somebody!" Nancy reported with as much consternation as she could pile onto the words. She stepped aside slightly so Michael could share the doorway with her.

Their father was caramel colored. He was slim and fit. He worked full-time (and a lot of overtime) at an Albertson's warehouse. He had been there for six years and was excited about a supervisor position he was close to obtaining. In the meantime his long hours at work and subsequent exhaustion when he got home kept him mostly in the dark, as far as his daughters were concerned. He still thought Cicely and Tanya were virgins.

"Girl, what in the world is wrong with you?" Michael asked his youngest child. "You got a week and a half to go, and this alternative school *mess* will be behind you. Are you telling me you can't make it? Are you serious right now?"

For the girls, nothing was worse than letting their father down. Cicely thought Tanya would give her up for sure now, but their sisterly bond was stronger than steel.

"I was just telling Cicely about something that happened at school," Tanya said. "But it wasn't me," she quickly added.

"You said you would beat the crap out of somebody," Nancy stated firmly. "I heard you."

"No, that's what this girl at school told another girl," Tanya lied. "I was telling Cicely what *they* said."

"And what makes you think Cicely needs to hear that?" Michael asked her. "It's not enough for you to be *corrupt*, but you wanna corrupt her too? She don't need to hear all of those damned war stories from your alternative school!"

"Um, I gotta hurry up and eat," Cicely said as she inched towards the door.

Her parents separated for a moment to let her pass.

"It's some waffles in the toaster," her mother told her.

Cicely looked back at her sister for a moment and apologized as best she could with her eyes before heading to the kitchen. The second she was gone, her parents reestablished their united front. Tanya had to endure their lecture for another two minutes.

CHAPTER ELEVEN
CONSEQUENCES

I could swoop a cute guy up
And make him my king...
I can't stop thinking of him
And one day
A wedding ring!
Why do I feel this way?
Is this the "Love" I have heard about?
No way...

I don't know what love is...

By Jasmine Walker

Cicely didn't get a chance to round up her homegirls on the way to school because her dad dropped her off. But she met up with Sandra, Toya and Serena in the cafeteria prior to the first bell. None of them knew what was going on, only that they were all included in a group text message Cicely sent twenty minutes ago. The message simply stated: Meet me in the cafeteria this morning. It's going down!

"What's up?" Toya asked when Cicely finally showed up. "I got your message, and I hit you back. Why didn't you answer?"

Cicely knew that all of her friends had replied to her ambiguous text.

"Sorry," she said. "My dad doesn't like me to be on the phone when we're in the car together."

"That's lame," Toya told her.

Cicely didn't reply, but she understood her dad's reasoning. With his heavy work schedule, every minute Michael got to spend with his family was valuable. He didn't want Cicely to ignore him during the ten minute ride to school.

"Y'all know who Alma Fuertes is?" Cicely knew they didn't, so she pulled up Facebook on her phone while her friends racked their brains. Alma was a nobody. Nobody paid her any attention.

"A Mexican girl?" Sandra asked.

"Duh," Toya said. "Obviously *Alma Fuertes* is Mexican."

"I have a class with her," Serena said. "What about her?"

Cicely had accessed the girl's profile by then. She clicked on one of her pics and handed the phone to Toya.

"That ho messaged me this morning," Cicely explained. "She said she's messing with Byron."

Toya frowned. Her heart was swiftly filled with malice. "This chick?"

Sandra leaned over her shoulder, so she could check out the picture, too.

"Hold up," Cicely said. She took the phone from them and pulled up the message feed. "Read it."

She stood quietly for a few moments while her friends analyzed the conversation.

Serena was the first to speak. Her pretty, brown eyes were dark with foreboding.

"What you gon' do?"

"Did you talk to Byron?" Toya asked.

"Yeah. He denied it," Cicely said.

"What about this picture?" Sandra asked, still looking at the phone.

"That ho can take a picture anywhere," Toya said.

"Byron said he met her at the park, and—"

"*At the park*? Hell naw. He's lying," Toya said.

"He said he was walking his dog, and he ran into her," Cicely continued. "She lives somewhere close to his house."

"So she asked him to take a picture, just because they saw each other?" Toya said that like it was the most ridiculous thing in the world.

Cicely was annoyed with her friend's interruptions, but she knew Toya was right. The story didn't make sense.

"No," she said. "They started talking. Supposedly Alma told Byron she liked him, and he told her he couldn't talk to her, because he was with me."

"So she took a picture?" Toya said. "Something to remember him by?"

"I don't know why she took that picture," Cicely grumbled. "But I'm gonna ask her today."

"What did Byron say?" Sandra asked again.

"I didn't ask him about the picture yet," Cicely reported. "He told me he shut her down, and that was it."

"Somebody's lying," Sandra deduced.

"Really?" Toya said. "You think?"

"What are you gonna do?" Serena asked.

113

"Me and Byron are gonna confront her together," Cicely said. "After that, it's whatever."

"You should bust her in the eye for lying," Toya said.

Cicely nodded. "Yeah, that's what I'm thinking."

"You know I got your back," Toya replied.

"Me, too," Sandra said.

"I'm not fighting nobody," Serena said.

Cicely would've been upset to hear that, if not for the fact that Serena was over three months pregnant. Only a hardcore hoodrat would disregard her baby's safety for a fight.

"You shouldn't fight her at school," Sandra advised her. "You don't want to get kicked out right before graduation."

"They can't kick you out," Toya said. "You already got all your credits."

"We can go down the street after school," Sandra suggested. "There's a park around the corner. That's where everybody goes to fight."

"That would be better anyway," Toya said. "Teachers always wanna break stuff up. But if they're not there, it can go on for as long as we want it to."

Cicely smiled nervously as her heart thumped hard and fast. She didn't like to fight. She felt she was much too pretty to roll around on the dirty ground. An ugly chick like Alma would probably be okay with getting pummeled, so long as she managed to mar Cicely's face with a couple of scratches.

But sometimes you simply have to fight – or at least that's what Cicely told herself. Now that her friends had pledged their commitment, it was impossible to deescalate the situation.

"We'll talk to her at lunch," Cicely said. "After Byron calls her a liar to her face, I'll tell her to meet me after school."

"Bet," Toya replied. "I hope she brings her friends, too."

Cicely hadn't considered the possibility that Alma might have a crew of her own. She was not deterred. She wouldn't let anybody push up on her man. And no group of girls at the school was badder than her clique.

● ● ● ● ● ●

Cicely sent Byron several text messages throughout the morning. He didn't respond to them. By third period, her nerves started to get the best of her. Use of cellphones was prohibited during class, but nearly every student at Finley High disregarded that rule, sometimes blatantly. The teachers were supposed to take up students' phones, if they caught them using them at the wrong time. But more often than not the teacher would simply tell them to put it away.

Maybe today was the day Byron decided to follow the rules. Maybe his teachers in first, second *and* third period were on the prowl, and he didn't have a chance to send Cicely a short text. She chose to believe that, because the alternative was he was simply ignoring her. It made her stomach hurt, to think he would do that.

By the time the bell rang at the end of third period, Cicely's nerves were nearly shot. She jumped to her feet and gathered her things, only to be reminded (quite rudely) by Mrs. Peete that, "The bell does not dismiss you in this class, Cicely. *I* do."

She sat back down and glared at the teacher while she gave them a few last minute instructions that went through one ear and out the other. When Mrs. Peete finally said, "Okay, Cicely, now you're dismissed," Cicely rolled her eyes and made it halfway down the aisle before Toya said, "Wait, girl. Don't forget about me!"

Cicely folded her arms over her chest as she stopped to wait on her. Next to Sandra, Toya was the most credible threat in their crew, so her presence was needed for any altercation, be it verbal or physical. But *jeez*, Toya seemed to be taking her sweet time today! Did she not know that Cicely's whole life was hanging in the balance? Either Byron had made a fool out of her, or Alma was flat-out lying, which seemed highly unlikely at this point. Either way Cicely had been waiting far too long for an answer. She felt like she was waiting on the results from a pregnancy test.

"You can't wait to see that girl, can you?" Toya said when she caught up with her.

"No," Cicely said. Her face was stone cold. Every muscle in her body was tense. "I can't."

"Let's go find her then."

"We gotta find Byron first," Cicely reminded her.

"Well let's go find him then."

As luck would have it, the girls didn't have to go far. They exited the classroom and headed for Cicely's locker, which was the closest. On the way there, Cicely thought she saw the love of her life down the hallway. Her heart was beating so fast, she felt light-headed. All of the blood drained from her face when she saw that Byron was not alone. He was walking with Alma!

Cicely hoped he brought her along to save them the trouble of tracking her down. But if that was the case, Alma would look scared or guilty, wouldn't she? She certainly wouldn't look like she'd won first prize at the county fair. Cicely saw that the whore's smile was evil and self-righteous, like Alma had all of the good cards in her deck, and she knew it.

"Is that ho holding his hand?" Toya asked.

Cicely found it hard to confirm that, because her eyes were now blurry with tears. She refused to believe Byron would do this to her. She loved him, and he said he loved her too. And Alma was so ugly! Her breasts were bigger than Cicely's, and her hips were curvier, but how could he get past that *face*? She had bug eyes and crooked teeth and a big, fat nose. Her hair was flat and dry and probably flea-infested.

When they were within ten feet, Cicely wiped her eyes and saw that none of her negative thoughts were true. Alma did in fact have big boobs and shapely hips, but she also had a beautiful face to go with it. Her hair was long and luxurious. Her makeup was perfect.

Cicely waited until Byron said, "Hey, uh, I'm sorry. I'm with her now," before she dropped everything in her hands and went after Alma with all ten claws extended. A second later both of her fists were full of that long, luxurious hair. She yanked it like it was a wig that would surely come off if she exerted enough pressure.

As Alma's screams filled her ears, Cicely barely felt someone rush in from the side and grab her own hair. They jerked so hard, Cicely's head was pulled all the way back, until she was looking up at the ceiling. She snarled as *another* assailant joined the fracas. This one started punching and kicking, but with the adrenaline rushing through her system, Cicely didn't feel those blows either.

"Get off her!"

She recognized that voice as Toya's. Cicely had never been so happy to have her friend by her side. She continued to wrench Alma's hair, while Toya went on the offense against her friends. Ten seconds later all five girls were on the floor, rolling and screaming, creating a huge, discombobulated mass of arms and legs and hair and feet. Somewhere in the midst of it, Cicely was able to get Alma on her back and fully mount her. She went to town on her pretty face; punching and slapping, hoping to inflict as much damage as she imagined Alma would've tried to inflict on her.

But it was all over much too soon.

Before the students' chants of, "*Fight! Fight!*" could make it to the cafeteria, Cicely felt strong, masculine hands pulling her off her prey. She knew it was a teacher, but she fought against him anyway, until he yelled very close to her ear, "*If you kick me again, you're going to jail!*"

As she was detached from Alma, Cicely saw Toya brawling with both of Alma's friends. And she was winning, too! Alma's homegirls were underclassmen, and they both looked scared to death, even though they had the numerical advantage.

The blood rushing past Cicely's ears sounded like a freight train. She saw everyone's lips moving, but she couldn't make out what they were saying. Alma made it to her feet and looked around wildly. Her face was fire engine red, her hairdo destroyed. When she spotted her nemesis, she charged like a mad bull, hoping to get in a few blows while Cicely was being restrained. Bad move. Cicely saw her coming and threw her leg up at the perfect moment. She landed a solid kick to Alma's stomach that sent the girl stumbling backwards, gasping for air.

The teacher holding Cicely (who she later learned was Coach Mitchell) took her continued aggression as a failure on his part. He yanked her back roughly and then spun unexpectedly, sending both of them falling to the floor. Cicely hit the tiles first, and Coach Mitchell came down on top of her. The pain she felt upon impact was real, and so was her scream. But Coach Mitchell wouldn't let her up – not until every student involved in the fight was restrained and everyone not involved was ushered away from the danger zone.

● ● ● ● ● ●

News of the brawl spread like a wildfire. By the end of the day every student at the school had heard a version of the wild event. Sandra, who didn't have time to meet up with her friends prior to the fight, had a whirlwind of emotions swirling through her heart and mind. The most poignant of them was survivor's guilt.

She and Serena had 7th period biology together. They were anxious to talk about what had happened, but they didn't have seats close to each other. Mrs. Peete was a stickler when it came to her seating chart.

When the intercom chimed for the afternoon announcements, all of the students began to put away their supplies. They were surprised to hear the principal on the intercom. Usually the job went to a student or one of the vice principals.

"Good afternoon," Mr. Walters said. "I hope you've all had a happy and productive day at Finley High. First of all, I would like to acknowledge all of the students who come to school to learn; the ones who take their education seriously.

I know you might not get a lot of praise – unless you're on the honor roll or you have perfect attendance. But if you're here to work, and you try your best every day, I want to commend you. All of you."

Sandra and Serena shot glances at each other across the classroom. Mr. Walters rarely went out of his way to praise middle-of-the-road students.

"As I'm sure you all know," the principal continued, "there was a fight on campus this morning. There were five students involved. We have a zero-tolerance policy for fighting in the Overbrook Meadows school district. None of the students involved in this morning's incident will return to this school for the rest of the year. Two of the students were juniors, and their suspensions will continue after the summer vacation, when classes resume in the fall."

Sandra expected that, but it broke her heart to know it was official: Toya and Cicely would not return to Finley High. They wouldn't get a chance to say goodbye to all of their teachers and friends; some of whom they'd known since grade school.

"As for the three *seniors* who were involved in the fight," Mr. Walters said, "none of them will walk the stage during our graduation ceremony next week."

Sandra's jaw dropped. Her eyes widened at the same pace. From the sudden murmurs that spread across the classroom, she knew she wasn't the only one who was surprised by that.

"A passing grade on the state exams might guarantee you a diploma," the principal continued. "But Finley High's graduation ceremony is a *privilege*. That is not something we have to offer you or something we're required to let you be a part of. It's not something you will be included in, if you don't carry yourselves like the smart, mature, capable young adults I know you are.

"Now, I was once a student in high school myself. I know how antsy seniors can get at this time of year. You're about to graduate. Many of you are going to college. You've got a lot of great plans for the future. But some of you have old scores you want to settle before you get out of here.

"Personally, I think you're too old for the notion of waiting till the last day of school to fight someone. But if that sounds like something you're interested in, please take my advice: *Don't do it.* Your graduation ceremony is a very big deal. Think about your family, before you deprive them of such a special occasion."

The principal ended the announcements abruptly. Sandra was too stunned to speak. She felt like everyone in the classroom was watching her, because Toya and Cicely were her best friends. When she looked around, she found that was indeed the case.

● ● ● ● ● ●

She and Serena left the classroom together. They were both quiet and contemplative, neither of them speaking for a while. Sandra felt like Toya and Cicely's fate hit her a little harder, because Serena had already begun to distance herself from her old running buddies.

When they got to her locker, Serena broke the silence by asking, "How come you weren't in it?"

"I wasn't there," Sandra explained. "Toya and Cicely had third period together. I was going to meet them in the cafeteria at lunch, but they never made it."

"If you were there, you would've been fighting too?"

Serena already knew the answer to that, so Sandra didn't bother responding. She looked down at her shoes and sighed.

"I thought Cicely was different," Serena revealed.

"Different how?" Sandra asked.

"I thought she was trying to stay out of trouble. She used to come to the bible club meetings," Serena told her. "She said she wanted to do right; make better decisions."

"Sometimes you don't have time to think about all that," Sandra said. "I heard everything happened real fast. Byron said he wanted to be with Alma, and all of a sudden everybody was fighting."

"Please don't believe that," Serena told her. "She already knew what she wanted to do. She was looking to fight that girl, and they ended up fighting. That's the way life is: When you're looking for trouble, you'll find it."

"So, what are you saying?" Sandra wondered. "She was just supposed to let that girl say whatever? Byron cheated on her and dissed her in front of everybody."

"You remember what happened to me at the prom?" Serena asked. "Jamar's sister embarrassed me way worse. But I didn't hit her. I turned and walked away. That was my choice."

"I hear what you're saying, but it's not always that easy."

"Trust me, I know. But fighting isn't worth it. And now Cicely and Toya are kicked out of school, and for what?"

Sandra nodded noncommittally.

"Are you gonna be okay for the next week and a half, without them around?" Serena wondered.

"I'll be alright."

"You know I'm here for you. It might be good for you to get away from some of that for a while."

That was the first time Serena had ever spoken negatively about Toya and Cicely. Sandra didn't know how to respond. She stood awkwardly, while Serena gathered the things she needed from her locker, and then she began to walk away.

"Wait," Serena said. "Are you walking home? Do you want me to walk with you?"

"No, my mom's coming," Sandra told her.

"Are you alright?"

Sandra nodded. And then she turned away from her, so Serena couldn't see the truth in her woeful eyes.

"Just need some time to think," Sandra said and continued down the hallway.

CHAPTER TWELVE
ADULT VS ADULT

Cicely's father had to leave work to retrieve her from school. He looked so forlorn, she dreaded getting into the car with him.

Michael didn't say much during the drive home, which was somehow worse than if he'd yelled at her. Cicely knew she wasn't the best daughter in the world, but she always tried to stay in his good graces. Every little girl wants her father to be proud of her.

When they neared their home, Michael finally broke eye contact with the road. Up to that point, his eyes were so fixated, Cicely wasn't sure if he was blinking or not.

He looked over at her and said, "Why, baby girl? Why were you fighting?"

His gaze made Cicely feel sick all over. She looked down at her hands in her lap. She shrugged.

"I don't know."

"Did she hit you first?" her father asked.

Cicely wanted to lie, but what was the point? A lie wouldn't get her out of any of the trouble she was in. She shook her head.

"Your friends put you up to this?" he asked. "That damned Toya..."

Cicely almost jumped at the chance to throw her friend under the bus. But that would only be a short-term fix. She and Toya planned to be friends forever. She didn't want her father to be any more wary of her than he already was.

She shook her head again.

Michael sighed. "So you attacked that girl, and you don't want to tell me why..."

Cicely's lips trembled, but she couldn't articulate a response. She attacked Alma because she was hurt and embarrassed. She knew that was asinine. No responsible parent would find that acceptable.

Michael shook his head as he pulled into the driveway. "I have to go back to work," he told her.

A wave of relief washed over Cicely. She didn't want to be home from school this early, but it wouldn't be so bad if she was alone. If her father stayed with her, she'd have to walk on eggshells for the next five hours; afraid to make any noise that sounded like she was enjoying herself.

She unbuckled her seatbelt and told him, "I'm sorry," as she got out of the car.

"Wait," he said before she closed the door. "Your mama said for me to take your cellphone."

Cicely's eyes widened. She had to use every muscle in her face to keep from showing the shock and horror she suddenly felt.

Take my phone? You might as well just kill me!

"What if, what if I need to call you?" she murmured.

That was the first excuse she could think of, and she knew it wouldn't work.

"You know we have a house phone," her father said.

Cicely began to pant noticeably. The thought of using such an antiquated device made her nauseous.

"Give it here," her father said, showing a glimpse of anger for the first time. "Hurry up. I gotta get back to work."

He leaned over the passenger seat and held out his hand. Cicely swallowed hard as she removed her cellphone from her back pocket. She felt like she was handing over one of her kidneys when she placed it in his hand.

Before she closed the door, Michael looked her in the eyes, and his demeanor softened again.

"I thought you were better than this," he told her.

His comment made Cicely feel lower than dirt – not only because she wasn't the good girl he thought she was, but also because she never had been. She'd been working hard to pull the wool over his eyes since middle school. Now her cover was blown.

She closed the car door and slowly made her way to the front porch. Her father didn't drive away until she made it inside safely.

● ● ● ● ● ●

Cicely went straight to her room and tossed her backpack on her bed. She stepped inside her closet and began to clear the shoes and other rubble from the carpeted floor. When she was done, she could barely make out a large, rectangular pattern cut into the carpet. On one side of the rectangle, she saw the tip of a Ziploc bag poking out.

She left the room in search of a screwdriver. A big one. She found it in the toolbox her father kept in the shed out back. When she returned to her closet, Cicely used the screwdriver to pry up the section of the floor. A long time ago, when they first moved into the house, her mother told her this hole was a *crawl space*.

The Ziploc bag was pinned perfectly with the cover of the hole. When she removed it, the bag fell to the bottom of the crawl space. Cicely cringed, as she always did when she had to reach down there. It was dark, and there might be a horde of red-eyed possums living under the house. The boogeyman himself might be waiting to grab her hand and pull her below.

She had to lie on her stomach to reach the bottom of the hole. When she pulled the baggie up, she saw that her stash was exactly as she left it. She put the lid back in place and returned all of her shoes to the closet. She sat on her bed and unzipped the baggie, and *voilà!* She had a cellphone.

This one was a cheap TracFone she bought from Family Dollar for thirty bucks. An additional twenty dollars got her 60 minutes of talk time. She had to use those minutes sparingly. The phone didn't have a data plan, so she couldn't access the internet, which was a major downside. But she could use it to call her friends; to make plans and plot and scheme.

The phone's battery was dead. Cicely found the charger and plugged it up. In the meantime, she powered-up her laptop. She knew her mother would confiscate that too when she got home. Until then, Cicely had to take care of some unfinished business.

She went to Facebook and saw that she had another personal message. She was surprised to find that it was from Alma:

Dumb ass. Got everybody in trouble

Cicely couldn't type her response fast enough.

U mad ho?

She went to Byron's page while she waited for a response. Cicely was so livid, she didn't bother sending him a personal message. He didn't deserve privacy. She wanted everyone to know what kind of creep he was, so she posted a message directly on his Facebook wall:

You had a good one. I was always there for you, but you wanna cheat on me with some ugly chick? Alright. They say you never know what you got until it's gone. You're going to find out what that means. You'll never have another girl like me. Hope you're happy with your thot.

Cicely backed out and checked her emails and then her newsfeed on Instagram and Twitter. When she was done, she went to the kitchen and plucked the house phone off the charger. She called her best friend. Toya's cellphone went straight to voicemail. Cicely expected that. Toya's mom wasn't very attentive, but she knew how to dole out punishments when they were due.

The only other people she wanted to talk to at the moment were Byron and Sandra. She didn't call Sandra because she was still in school. She should have the ringer turned off on her cellphone, but Cicely didn't want to get her in trouble if she forgot to do so. She didn't show Byron the same consideration. She didn't care if he forgot to turn his ringer off and a teacher confiscated his phone. But that call went straight to voicemail too.

When she got back to her laptop, Cicely was excited to see that Alma was ready for a cyber-war. Not only did the whore respond to Cicely's personal message, but she also commented on the post Cicely left on Byron's wall:

"Get over it ho! You not that pretty. You skinny and you ugly. Byron don't want you! Move on boo boo! Next time you wanna fight, we don't have to do it at school. You can come see me anytime! We can go to the park right now! Whack ass ho!"

Cicely's mouth hung open when she was done reading. Her face flushed with heat. She couldn't believe Alma wanted to put so much of their business in the open like that. She supposed she deserved it, to a certain degree. But her initial comment to Byron was tasteful. She didn't mention Alma by name, and she wasn't being disrespectful.

Alma, on the other hand, had taken it to another level. She wanted everyone to know who she was and what had happened at school today. Cicely considered ignoring her, but that would mean defeat. The people on Facebook had no idea what was going on. She'd be damned if they only got Alma's side of the story.

Rather than go back to their personal messages, she continued the argument on Byron's wall:

"You still talking noise after I yanked most of your hair out? We already know you ain't trying to see me like that again."

Alma must've been waiting, because her response came within seconds:

"I still got all my hair. Not one bruise on my face."

"Take a pic ho. We need proof."

"Why dont you take a pic! You the one got jumped!"

"Not a stain on me. Your little friends didn't do nothing! Ran up and got that ass whooped. Just like you! How's your stomach? Hope you wasn't pregnant!"

"I dont feel no pain ho. But Byrons gonna rub it for me tonite"

"Good luck with that! He ringing my line right now. But you can have him! Hos need to stick together"

"I can have him? Lol. You kno you want him. U mad ho? Yep, this ho mad."

The truth of that barb cut deeply. Cicely lost all sense of civility, and the conversation thread became darker and darker. She started dropping F-bombs like they were candy. Alma matched her vulgarity word by word. They called each other every vile thing imaginable. By the time they were done, twenty minutes had passed, and they had posted more than sixty comments in all. In the end, they agreed to meet up again for part two of their interrupted rumble.

When she closed her laptop, Cicely was so angry she wanted to throw the computer across the room. Instead she screamed and pounded her bed with hammer fists. She couldn't wait to see Alma again. Her mind was filled with images of her bloody face.

In the meantime she was in desperate need of a stress reliever. She found half a blunt in one of her winter coats. It was sealed in a freezer bag, but Cicely still found the odor rather pungent. She went to the backyard and sat under her favorite tree and smoked until the drama didn't seem so bad at all.

• • • • • •

Her mom got home a little after six. She would've been there sooner, but she had to pick Tanya up from the alternative school. Tanya was eager to run to her sister's room to get the scoop about the fight, but Nancy beat her to it.

"Tell me what the hell happened."

Unlike her father, who kept his emotions under wraps for the most part, her mother was a hellcat. She looked like she might physically assault her if she lied, so Cicely opted for a version of the truth. She told her how Alma started the beef on Facebook this morning, and she said Alma initiated the confrontation when they got to school.

"So that was *you* Tanya was talking about," Nancy deduced. "This morning we got on Tanya's case about fighting, but it was you the whole time..."

Cicely sat on her bed. She looked pale and very skinny. She brought a hand to her mouth and started chewing on her pinkie nail.

"You let me and your father yell at her, *knowing it was you...*" Nancy continued. Her big chest rose and fell with each of her heavy breaths. "You had a chance to tell us you had a problem, Cicely. But you didn't! You walked right out of this house and decided to settle it yourself..."

Cicely's eyes darted, but unless she was willing to bowl her mother over, there was nowhere to go.

"You know you're not graduating, right?" Nancy asked.

Cicely couldn't hide her surprise. They couldn't do that. It was only a fight.

"You'll get your funky diploma," her mother said. "But you're not walking across that stage. Your grandmother was going to get on a plane for the first time to see that. All of your aunts and uncles were gonna be there. But that's gone! You lost *everything*."

Nancy's throat caught. She wore a pained expression. Cicely's eyes filled with tears. She began to stutter something that was unintelligible.

"My boss called the school," Nancy informed her. "He called the superintendent, too." She shook her head. "He couldn't do nothing. You're not walking across that stage."

Cicely's tears flowed freely. Her mom worked for an attorney. If he couldn't do anything about it, then the decision really was final. Out of all of the horrible things that happened today, this had to be the worst. Cicely had been dreaming about her graduation ceremony for months.

"Where's your laptop?" Nancy asked, her anger back in place. She looked around and spotted it on the desk.

Cicely expected to lose that, so she didn't react. But what her mother said next shook her to the very core.

"Turn it on," Nancy instructed. "Pull up Facebook. I wanna see what this girl said to you that was worth you losing everything."

Cicely remained frozen in place as memories of the comments she'd posted filled her head. The personal messages were bad enough. There was no way she could let her mom see the stuff she wrote on Byron's wall.

"*Did you hear what I said?!*" Nancy barked.

"*Mama, please,*" Cicely blubbered.

Nancy's eyes widened for a moment and then narrowed. "Oh, it's that bad, huh?"

She made a move for the laptop. Cicely stood to stop her. Her mother turned on her with a look in her eyes that made Cicely sit back down. Quickly. Nancy stared her down for a few moments, daring her to stand again, and then she took a seat at the desk.

Cicely sat quietly for the next five minutes, crying and wringing her hands in her lap. Her mother didn't speak as she read her personal messages with Alma. Nancy had a Facebook account herself, so she knew how to check her daughter's news feed. She sucked air through her teeth when she saw the humongous conversation thread on Byron's wall. She read the whole thing. Each line caused her breathing to become more labored.

Cicely cowered under her countenance. She was reduced to a pile of trembling bones by the time Nancy turned away from the computer and faced her again. She stared at her for so long, Cicely felt like her mom could see all the way to her wicked soul.

Nancy finally shook her head and asked, "Who the hell are you?"

Cicely didn't know how to answer that. She knew she'd been living a double-life of sorts. There was the good girl her parents knew, and then there was the hood girl her friends at school knew. She didn't plan for these two worlds to collide. She knew she was driving her parents crazy right now.

"You are not my daughter," Nancy breathed. "This person..." She waved a hand at the laptop screen. "I don't know who this person is, but I don't like her. The sad thing is, I know that's who you really are on the inside. The person me and your father thought you were... That's the one who was only pretending."

Cicely shook her head in denial, and then she stood suddenly when her mother turned back to the computer. Nancy was not worried in the slightest.

"Girl, if you're thinking about hitting me, you'd better make it a good one."

Cicely hadn't planned to do that at all, but she couldn't sit calmly while her mother took hold of the mouse and made adjustments to her personal information.

"Wha, what are you doing?" she asked when Nancy clicked on Settings.

"I'm changing your password. You're suspended from Facebook."

"Wait. You can't do that!"

Her mother rose to her feet and took a step forward, until they were chest to chest.

"Stop me then."

Nancy weighed twice as much as her daughter. Cicely didn't know why she was trying to bait her into a physical confrontation. She wasn't crazy enough to raise a hand to her mother.

"I'm not gonna fight you, Mama!"

"Then sit your little ass down and shut up."

"But you can't block me off Facebook! I'm eighteen! You can't do me like that anymore!"

"I can't? Girl, who the hell you talking to?" Nancy asked. She continued talking before Cicely could reply. "You think you grown? Then get a job and move out! Go on. Go be grown!"

She waited. After no one made a move, Nancy said, "Well, if you're not ready to move out, then you must not be that grown, huh? So until you're ready for that, you do what the hell I say. And you will respect the rules in my house! *I* bought your phone. *I* pay the phone bill. *I* pay the cable bill. I bought this damned laptop, and I pay for the internet! You can't even drink a glass of water in this house without depending on me to provide it!"

She waited for a rebuttal. Cicely had none.

"She done lost her damn mind..." Nancy muttered as she turned back to the laptop.

Rather than change the password in front of her, she picked it up and left the room with it. Cicely knew better than to speak again. She stood flustered for a few seconds before she returned to her seat on the bed.

Three minutes later she was curled in a fetal position, crying over lost love, lost trust and her graduation ceremony, which had also been taken away.

CHAPTER THIRTEEN
SCHEMING

Please tell me, does he meet your needs?
My boyfriend, does he speak of me?
His soft lips, do they still taste sweet?
Or do they only lie? Dream
Of darkness, deadly shadows. Dream
Of fury, keen and focused. Streams
Of terror that bombard your dreams

-KTW

At ten o'clock that night Sandra received a call from a number she didn't recognize. When she answered, the caller barely spoke above a whisper.

"Hello?"

"Hey."

"Hello?"

"Sandra. It's me, Cicely."

"Who?"

"*Cicely.*"

"Oh. What, what's up, girl? Why you whispering?"

"I'm in the closet. I can't talk loud right now."

"Why?"

"Why you think? My mama took my phone."

"Is this that cheap TracFone you bought?"

"Yeah."

"I didn't know you still had it."

"I save it for emergencies," Cicely told her.

"Oh. Is everything... I mean, are you okay?"

"No. Not really."

"They said you can't graduate with us."

"I know. My mama told me."

"That's messed up," Sandra said. "They shouldn't kick y'all out of graduation for fighting."

"Yeah, well, it's over now. My mama said there's nothing I can do about it."

"You don't have your laptop?" Sandra asked. "I been trying to message you on Facebook."

"No. My mama took it. And she changed my password, so stop sending me messages. If somebody replies to you, it's not me."

"Man, that's messed up."

"I know," Cicely said.

"Have you talked to Toya?"

"No. Have you?"

"Yeah. I talked to her about an hour ago. She said she can't get in contact with you, either. She said she called your house phone, and your mom hung up on her."

"Toya still has her cellphone?"

"Yeah."

Cicely couldn't believe it. She couldn't help but feel jealous.

"Can you call her on three-way?"

"Yeah," Sandra said. "Hold on a second."

Cicely waited in the darkness of her closet. Both of her parents were home, but she thought her dad had gone to bed already. He never had a lot of energy at the end of a workday. Her mother was probably still awake, but Nancy had been giving her the silent treatment since their big argument. Cicely doubted if she would come to give her a goodnight kiss.

There were no warning clicks before her friends were back on the line.

"Hello?"

"Yeah, I'm still here," Cicely said.

"Girl, what the hell is going on with you?" Toya bellowed.

"I'm on punishment."

"They took your phone and your laptop?"

"Yeah. Got me using this ugly TracFone. I can't even get on the internet."

"Damn. Sucks to be you," Toya said.

"Yes, it does," Cicely agreed. "How do you still have your phone?"

Toya smacked her lips. "Girl, please. I'm nineteen years old. What is she gonna do, bend me over her knee and give me a spanking?"

"No, but I thought you'd get grounded like me."

"I'm nineteen years old," Toya reiterated. "I'm an *adult*. My mama knows she can't punish me like I'm a kid or something. Plus she thinks missing out on graduation is punishment enough."

Cicely agreed with that. She wished she had a mother like Toya's.

"She didn't punish you at all?" she asked.

"My mama doesn't pay my phone bill," Toya informed her. "And she didn't buy my phone. I'll call the police, if she tries to take it."

"Who bought your phone?" Cicely wondered.

"Trayshaun."

Cicely recognized the name as one of Toya's previous boyfriends.

"Who pays the bill?"

"Derrick paid it last month. I'll find somebody to pay for it this month. It's only fifty dollars."

"That sucks."

"Why? You want me to be stuck out like you?"

"No," Cicely conceded. "But I don't wanna be the only one in trouble."

"I'm in trouble too," Toya assured her. "I can't go back to school, and I don't get to graduate either."

"I can't believe y'all won't be at graduation," Sandra chipped in.

"Girl, I saw you going *HAM* on Facebook," Toya said with a laugh.

"Did Byron ever respond?" Cicely wondered.

"Hell naw. But he didn't delete it, either."

"He probably thinks it's cool to have two girls fighting over him," Sandra guessed.

"Probably," Toya agreed.

"Are you alright?" Cicely asked, thinking about the fight at school.

"Who?" Sandra asked.

"Toya."

"Me? Yeah. Why you say that?"

"I saw those girls try to jump you."

"Oh. Naw, I'm fine. You might wanna ask them if *they're* alright, though. I handled both them ho's."

"I'm sorry," Cicely said. "I didn't mean to get you caught up in that. It happened so fast."

"So Byron did cheat on you?" Sandra asked.

"Yeah," Toya said. "He said so hisself."

"With *Alma*?" Sandra found that hard to believe. Cicely was the prettiest girl she knew in real life. Alma was only moderately attractive. Alma may have had a better figure, but Cicely was the whole package.

"She must be a slut," Toya guessed.

"I know she is," Cicely said. "That's the only thing it could be. She probably gave him some when she saw him at the park."

"Outside?" Sandra asked.

"A ho will get down *anywhere*," Cicely said. "Outside, inside, in the bathroom at school. It don't matter."

"But you had sex with him, too," Sandra said. "What was she doing that you wouldn't do?"

Cicely couldn't think of anything offhand. She had done things for Byron that she'd never done for anyone else.

"It don't matter," Toya said. "What we need to figure out is how we gon' get at her."

"She already said she wants to fight again," Sandra said. "So it's whatever."

"I know," Cicely replied. "I wish I still had my computer, so I could set something up."

"She said she was gon' get you, if you show up at William's party," Sandra reported.

Cicely's eyes widened. "Who said that?"

"Alma did. She told Bethany and some more people."

Cicely was suddenly enraged again. "Are you serious? That ho knows she's not trying to see me."

"Yeah," Sandra said. "But you won't be able to go to the party, will you?"

"Oh, I'll find a way to get to that party," Cicely said definitively.

"You *gotta* go," Toya said, "especially since we're not going to graduation. That party is the last chance we'll have to hang out with the seniors."

"Everybody wants to see y'all, at least one more time," Sandra agreed.

Cicely's mind raced. The party was already important to her, but now it was a necessity. The way she and Toya were unceremoniously removed from Finley High was a tragedy that would haunt them for years to come. Being excluded from graduation added salt to the wound. Cicely believed she deserved a chance to say goodbye to her high school friends. No adult should take that away from her.

She hoped that when she explained this to her mother, Nancy would agree and take her off punishment, just for one night. She didn't need her cellphone back right now, and she could live without her laptop, too. But William's party was a *must*.

Unfortunately the party was only two days away. Today was already wasted, so that left one day for Cicely to be the best, most remorseful daughter she could be. After a day of perfect behavior, she would tell her mom about the party. If Nancy wouldn't let her go, well, there was always the bedroom window. She hadn't sneaked out in over a year, but drastic times called for drastic measures.

"I'll be at that party," she assured her friends.

141

"Awesome!" Toya said. "I already picked out my bikini!"

"Hey, I gotta go," Cicely said. "I don't have a lot of minutes left on this phone."

"Dang," Toya said. "They got you over there counting your phone minutes like a hobo."

"Everybody's not able to have a bunch of sugar daddies," Cicely told her.

"Yes. You are," Toya said earnestly. "You're just not applying yourself."

"Bye, girl."

CHAPTER FOURTEEN
THE REPRIEVE

When I was in middle school
I was really shy
I didn't talk to anyone
Literally, no lie
That all changed when I got to high school
"You don't smoke? Girl, you a fool"

By Friday things remained tense at Cicely's home, but it wasn't as bad as Wednesday. Rather than allow her and Toya to stay home for the seven days left in the school year, the powers that be required them to go to an alternative school. Piedmont was just as miserable as Tanya had been telling Cicely, but with her sister and her best friend there, it wasn't so bad.

Cicely knew she wouldn't learn anything in the short time she had to attend. That was fine because her new teachers didn't seem interested in teaching. Much like the students, they appeared to be going through the motions. They too had already started the countdown for summer vacation.

Because of their grade difference, Cicely and Tanya didn't have any classes together at Piedmont. They only saw each other at lunchtime and after school, while they waited for their mother to pick them up. At four o'clock that afternoon the sisters dallied near the main entrance, while most of the other students boarded their buses. Tanya wanted to get Cicely's opinion about a boy she had a crush on, but Cicely had more pressing matters to discuss.

"I think I'm gonna sneak out tonight."

Tanya was instantly wary. Cicely wasn't normally the type to be so reckless.

"Why? Where you trying to go?"

"A party," Cicely said. She told her about William's get-together and what it had come to mean to her and her friends.

"Don't do it," Tanya advised her.

Cicely was surprised to hear that from her. Tanya's reputation of being a bad girl was well-earned.

"Why not?"

"What if Mama gets scared and calls the police?"

"She's not gonna call the cops, just because I snuck out."

"If you don't have your cellphone – *which you don't* – and she has no way to reach you, she might," Tanya said.

Cicely shook her head. "Maybe if I don't make it back by one or two in the morning, she might. But she won't call them right away."

"Plus she changed your password on Facebook," Tanya said.

Cicely frowned, not knowing what that had to do with anything.

"Just because you're locked out of your account, doesn't mean she is," Tanya explained. "She can log in as you and read everything your friends are posting. If everybody is talking about the party, it won't be hard to put two and two together and figure out where you are. You don't want her to come and drag you out of that boy's house. That would be embarrassing as hell."

Cicely's eyes widened, not because of the embarrassment factor, but because she hadn't considered the fact that Facebook could indeed sabotage her.

"You're right," she muttered. "That's why you're so sneaky; because you think of everything."

"If I did, I wouldn't get caught so much," Tanya acknowledged.

Cicely nodded. "What you think I should do then?"

Tanya shrugged. "I don't know. Ask her if you can go."

"She won't let me go," Cicely said with a shake of her head.

"If you explain it to her like you explained it to me, she might."

Cicely doubted that, but with little recourse, she figured it was worth a shot.

When their mother pulled into the school's parking lot ten minutes later, she hopped in the front seat and fixed doleful eyes on her.

"Hi, mom."

Nancy was immediately suspicious.

"What girl? What trouble you got yourself into now?"

"Nothing, Mama. I didn't do anything wrong."

"The hell you didn't," Nancy said. "I'm picking up *both* of my kids from the same alternative school. Do you

145

know how embarrassing that is? I'm sure my boss thinks I'm the worst parent ever."

Nancy sneered at the road as she exited the parking lot and merged into traffic. Seeing that she wouldn't be able to sweeten her up, Cicely tried a more direct approach. The worst her mom could say was *No*, in which case she would fall back on her original plan to sneak out.

"Mama, I know this is going to sound crazy, but I need to go to a party tonight."

Nancy took her eyes off the road long enough to look at her like she was crazy.

"I know I'm grounded," Cicely said, "but this is really important – especially since I can't go to graduation..." She gave her the spiel about seeing some of her friends for the last time and recapturing the opportunity to tell them goodbye and good luck with their future endeavors.

"I know it's my fault I got kicked out of school," she concluded. "I got in a fight, and I deserve to get punished. I understand why they kicked us out of graduation. I'm not asking you to take me off punishment. I'm not even asking for my phone back. I just need to go out *this one time*, and you can put me back on lockdown as soon as I get home. Please, Mama. I'll do anything..."

Nancy was by no means a softy when it came to parenting. Her initial reaction was to tell her daughter the request was absolutely absurd. But she took a moment to look at things from both sides. She didn't know if Cicely meant what she said about the graduation punishment being just, but Nancy did not agree with that at all. In fact, she was still considering suing the school district for such an over-the-top punishment. Her daughter got into *one* fight. How do you ban a student from their rightfully owed graduation ceremony for such a small offense?

And Nancy had fond memories of her senior year of high school. The friendships that were forged there may seem flippant to a lot of parents, but sometimes they were anything but. Nancy was married to her high school sweetheart. She and Michael had built a wonderful life together. It all started their junior year at Finley High.

She sighed and told Cicely, "Alright. You can go."

Cicely was stunned. She was planning her escape route, even as her mother mulled it over.

"Really?"

"Yes, girl. You did screw up your graduation. And you let a lot of people in the family down. But you made good grades at that school for four years. Taking away your chance to say goodbye to your friends is something that will affect you, for who knows how long. No punishment should be that severe."

The bright smile that spread across Cicely's face made Nancy's heart flutter. Her daughter was so beautiful, and she was a good kid, deep down. Every girl made a fool of herself over a boy at some point in their lives. She hoped Cicely had learned her lesson early and wouldn't continue to make terrible decisions when she was in her twenties and thirties.

"I'm going to let you take my car," Nancy added.

Cicely was floored by that news. Never in a million years did she think this conversation would go so smoothly. She couldn't articulate a response.

Nancy smirked at her.

"Don't get too excited," she said. "If you knew what me and your father were going to give you for graduation, you'd be crying right now. That's not including what you would've got from your grandmother and everyone else who came to the ceremony. Since you're not getting any of those gifts, using my car tonight is a pretty small concession."

At the moment, Cicely didn't care about the gifts she'd lost out on. The important thing was she was attending the party of the year tonight, and she'd get to drive her friends there to boot. This was like Christmas and her birthday, all rolled into one!

"Can I have my cellphone back, just for tonight?" she dared to ask. Why not? She was obviously on a roll. "In case there's an emergency..." she quickly added.

Nancy was so against giving the phone back, she almost reneged on the whole thing. But Cicely was right: You can't give a teenager the keys to your car unless they also have a way to contact you in case of an emergency.

"Yes, Cicely – *but just for tonight*," she growled, her mean countenance back in place.

Cicely continued smiling. She didn't care about her mother switching back to angry mom. The deal was done.

Tanya sat quietly in the backseat with her mouth wide open. Even though she witnessed the conversation, she had no idea how Cicely pulled this one off. Their mother would *never* have given in to her so easily.

Life was so unfair!

● ● ● ● ● ●

When they got home Cicely tried to play it cool for a while, but there was much planning to do. She waited thirty minutes before she summoned the courage to enter her mom's room and retrieve her cellphone. Nancy already said she could have it, but Cicely worried that she would wait

148

until she was ready to leave for the party before she actually handed it over.

Her mother had mostly undressed and was about to get in the shower. She asked her, "Why do you need it now?"

"I wanted to tell a few people I was going to make it to the party." Cicely fidgeted in the doorway. "Would it be alright if I picked up Sandra and... them?"

Her mother's eyes narrowed. "Them *who*? Toya?"

Cicely swallowed hard as she nodded.

"Girl, you're making me want to cancel this whole thing..." She shook her head. "Close the door."

Confused, Cicely backed out of the room and closed the door. Her mother opened it a few moments later and handed her the cellphone.

"Don't want you knowing where my hiding spots are," she said and closed the door again.

Cicely grinned as she hurried back to her room. Her mother was so silly. Cicely already knew where her hiding spots were!

Three hours later she left the house at 8 pm wearing shorts and sandals with a tasteful tee-shirt. She had her bikini hidden under the outfit. She couldn't wait to shed the tee-shirt and show off her boobs and flat stomach. Her father was home by then. His weekend had officially started, and he was in a good mood.

He told her, "Have fun, baby girl."

"Thanks, Dad!"

"Don't forget, you're back on punishment when you get home!" her mother yelled as she exited the house.

"I know!" Cicely replied. She closed the door and was 100% parent free for the next five hours.

It was hard to believe how fortunate she was. Her mother drove a 2011 Nissan Pathfinder. It was in great condition, and it had a nice audio system. When she slid behind the wheel and started the car, Cicely could no longer hold a burst of elated laughter. She was still giggling half a mile down the road, when she turned onto the main thoroughfare.

● ● ● ● ● ●

Twenty minutes later Toya asked her, "Girl, how the hell did you pull this off?" as she hopped in the back seat of the truck.

Sandra was already sitting pretty in the passenger seat. Cicely picked her up first, because she lived closer.

"I don't know," Cicely said honestly. Her smile was perky and sinful. She had the new Nicki Minaj CD in the changer. The girls were already crunk. "I just asked her," she said. "I didn't think she'd let me out, but she did!"

"And she gave you the car, too?" Toya exclaimed. "Man, you know it's going down tonight!"

Sandra turned towards the backseat. "You got your swimsuit?"

"Hell yeah!" Toya said. She had her hair freshly styled. Her makeup made her look like she was in her mid-twenties. Eyebrows on fleek. "And you know I got this too..." she boasted as she removed a plastic water bottle from her purse. The liquid inside the bottle was cherry red.

"What's that?" Cicely asked, dividing her attention between the road and the rearview mirror.

Toya held it up for her to see. "It's Kool-Aid and *vodka*. Mostly Kool-Aid..."

Sandra shook her head. "Mostly?"

"Sweet!" Cicely beamed. "I can't drink till I get to the party, though."

"That stuff's nasty," Sandra told them.

"Nuh-uhn. Not with Kool Aid," Toya promised her. "Are you gonna try it?"

Sandra shrugged. Her smile was curious now. "Maybe."

"You gon' learn today!" Toya belted.

They all laughed.

"Did you get the green?" Toya asked.

"Yeah, but I only got two blunts," Cicely told her. "They're in my purse. Get 'em, Sandra."

Sandra hefted her friend's purse and dug through it until she found the cigars. "You want both of them?"

"No, just light one of them."

Sandra's eyes widened. "Who? *Me*?"

"You said you were gonna smoke," Cicely reminded her.

"Here," Toya said. She reached from the backseat and handed her a lighter. "Light it up, girl!"

Sandra giggled nervously as she took the lighter and brought the blunt to her lips. Everyone became quiet until she lit it and took her first little puff. Her friends laughed when she coughed out the foul air.

"Hold it in," Cicely advised her. "If you blow it out too fast, you're wasting it."

Sandra tried again, but her lungs started burning when she held her breath. Again she coughed up most of the smoke.

"Damn, she really did it!" Toya exclaimed.

"You about to be in a whole 'nother world!" Cicely told her. She rolled down both of the front windows, and the thick plumes of smoke quickly dissipated.

"Here," Sandra said, offering the blunt to Toya.

"No, give it to me," Cicely said, intercepting it.

"You can smoke and drive?" Sandra wondered. Her eyes were watery, and her throat hurt a little from coughing.

"We'll be at the party by the time it kicks in," Cicely assured her.

"Have you talked to Byron?" Toya asked from the backseat. "Is he coming?"

"Nope. I haven't talked to him," Cicely said, her smile suddenly gone. "Forget that dude."

"You haven't asked him about Alma?" Sandra wondered.

"No. I didn't wanna waste my minutes on him."

Sandra watched her friend take two long pulls on the blunt and hold the smoke in for more than five seconds.

"Didn't you get your cellphone back?" Toya asked her. "Why don't you call him now? I wanna see what that fool has to say."

Cicely shrugged. She hit the blunt again before passing it to the backseat. "Alright. Whatever. Say, don't leave no ashes back there!"

"I won't!" Toya promised.

Cicely handed Sandra her cellphone. "Here. Call him. Put him on speaker."

Sandra grinned as she searched for Byron's number in her contacts. When the phone started to ring, she put the call on speaker and told Cicely, "Turn the radio down!"

Cicely turned it off altogether. The girls barely quieted down enough to hear Byron when he answered.

"Hello? Hello, Cicely?"

"Be quiet! *Be quiet*!" she told her friends. "Hey, what's up?" she said to her ex-boyfriend.

Sandra held the phone up, so Cicely could keep both hands on the wheel.

"Hey, what's going on?" he said. He never sounded more unsure of himself. "Am I on speaker? Who's with you?"

"Don't worry about all that!" Cicely snapped. "I wanted to know if you were coming to William's party tonight."

"Oh, uh, no. I'm at work right now," Byron said. "Hold on, let me go over here for a second..."

"Where he work?" Toya asked while they were on hold.

"McDonalds," Cicely said.

"*Flipping burgers*!" Toya said and laughed. "Here," she said, passing the blunt back to the front.

Sandra took it and tried to take it slow this time, so she wouldn't cough so hard.

"Cicely?" Byron said. "Baby, what's going on? Who is that?"

"I said don't worry about all that!" she quipped. "And don't call me *baby*, neither. I'm not your baby!"

Her friends laughed.

"Alright. If you wanna do it like this, I guess it is what it is," Byron grumbled. "I'm sorry for what happened with Alma. I don't wanna be with her. I don't know what I was thinking. I wanna be with you, Cicely."

"Boy, please," she said with a smack of her lips.

"I didn't cheat on you."

"Yes you did! You know you did. But it's all good."

"Okay, but you cheated on me *first!*" Byron reminded her. "With Steve."

That comment hurt Cicely more than she could let on. She was glad to have her friends there to give her the courage to stand up to him.

"That was a long time ago."

"It was only two months ago!"

"You said you forgave me."

"I did. I do!"

"Then why you bringing it up now, like that's the reason you did what you did?"

"I didn't mean it like that."

"You know what, it don't even matter no more. All I wanna know is if Alma's gonna be at the party tonight, 'cause I got something for that ho!"

"Oh yeah, she gotta pay," Toya agreed.

"What? Who is that, Toya?" Byron asked.

"Don't worry about it!" Toya shouted from the backseat.

"Cicely, please don't do that," Byron pleaded. "It's over. You said so yourself."

"So that ho *is* gon' be there," Cicely deduced.

"I don't know!" Byron said. "I haven't talked to her since Wednesday. I told you, I'm not with her!"

"Whatever. Hang up on that fool!" she told Sandra.

Her friend readily complied. The girls laughed as Cicely turned the tunes back on.

"Gimme my blunt," she said and took it from Sandra.

Toya told her, "You shouldn't have told him we were gonna get Alma. He'll probably warn her, and she won't come."

"It don't matter," Cicely said between puffs. "I just wanna have fun tonight. If she comes, I'll get her. If not, I'm still getting turnt!"

"You got some of these?" Toya asked. She produced more goodies from her purse. This time it was a 3-pack box of condoms.

"No," Cicely said. Her eyes were dazzling. "You think I should stop and get some?"

"You can have one of mine, if you need it," Toya said. "You think you might need the other one?" she asked Sandra. "Derrick and Chris are supposed to come."

Sandra smiled and blushed.

"No, I think she might need hers for *Peter*," Cicely said with a laugh.

"Peter? Peter *Scott*?" Toya asked.

"Yeah, that's her new boo-thang," Cicely informed her.

"No, it's not," Sandra countered.

"Uh-oh! I didn't know about that!" Toya squawked. "You definitely need to get you some of this," she said, passing the bottle of *mostly Kool-Aid* to the front. "That way you won't chicken out again. Pass the blunt!" she told Cicely.

Cicely reluctantly gave her the blunt as Sandra took the bottle. She gazed upon the concoction's soft, red tint. She removed the cap and brought the top to her nose and took a whiff. It smelled strong. And sweet. She looked over at Cicely, wondering if she would offer any opposition.

But Cicely said, "It's our last senior party. *Forever*. Might as well turn up!"

"Yeah, might as well!" Toya agreed. "Go on, girl! *Peer pressure!*"

Cicely laughed. Sandra did too. She couldn't believe she actually said the words *peer pressure*. That made the

155

whole idea of drinking and smoking even more taboo. Undeniably so.

Sandra looked to Cicely again for one last chance for guidance. Her friend grinned and said, "Go for it. Just for tonight. You high yet?"

Sandra shrugged. Everything was happening so fast, she didn't know what she was feeling. She grinned. No one noticed her smile was a little forced. She had a vision of her mother standing before her, looking angry. She blinked a few times, and her mother was gone.

Just for tonight, she told herself, and with a giggle she took a sip. The liquor was strong, but not as nasty as she expected. When she swallowed, her chest burned, so there was no doubt she was drinking alcohol. But with the Kool Aid, the vodka seemed far removed from its basic form.

"*Turn up!*" Toya cackled from the back seat.

Sandra laughed, and she took another sip. It was more of a drink this time, in the spirit of togetherness.

CHAPTER FIFTEEN
THE PERV

I wasn't respected at first
Lunchtime was just the worst
When I tried to make friends
The crowds would disperse
"Don't hang with her, she's just a baby"
Dang, I should smoke?
I don't know. Maybe

When they made it to William's house at nine pm, the party was fully underway. There were cars lining the street in both directions. Cicely had to park her mother's car on another block, but she wasn't worried about anyone bothering it. William lived in a well-to-do community; the kind with Neighborhood Watch signs posted in nearly every yard.

The girls left their tee-shirts in the car, so their cleavage and midriffs were on full display when they made it to William's front door. They heard music and laughter coming from inside before he opened it.

"Hey." William looked surprised to see them.

"Hey, William," Cicely said. "I see you already got things rolling!" She looked over his shoulder, but none of the guests were chilling in the foyer.

"I didn't think you would make it," he said. "You either," he told Toya.

"Why?" Toya asked him. "Just because we got suspended?"

"Well, yeah," he said.

"The principal can't stop us from going to a party," Cicely told him good-naturedly.

"I think Alma's coming," William said. "I invited her, too." He shook his head warily. "I don't want any trouble between y'all tonight. I can't have any fights here..."

"We're not gonna mess with that girl," Toya promised him. "That's over with."

"I'm not, I don't think I should let her come now, since y'all got here first," he decided.

"Whatever," Toya said. "Are you gonna let us in or not?"

She stood up straight and pushed her shoulders back, which just so happened to thrust her breasts towards his face. William couldn't help but look down at them. Sandra knew there was no way he would turn away three fine girls in bikinis and booty shorts.

"Yeah, sure," he said and stepped aside. "Y'all look great, by the way."

"Thank you!" the girls said as they entered his home.

Sandra looked back and caught him staring at their butts as he closed the door. He didn't try to hide it. His eyes were wide, his smile approving. She laughed and took another swig of her punch as they rounded the corner and were immersed in the party scene.

● ● ● ● ● ●

Williams' home was an aesthetic masterpiece. It was the kind of house Sandra always dreamed a prince would whisk her off to after he slayed the ferocious dragon. All of the furniture looked like it was fresh from the showroom. Each room looked like it had been put together by a designer. Even the paintings on the walls matched the curtains, which matched the floors and the furniture.

There was an entertainment center in the living room with thousands of dollars' worth of electronics perfectly arranged. The music from the living room flowed throughout the house via unseen speakers that were mounted in every room. The upstairs portion of the home was off-limits for the party, but that wasn't a problem. There was enough room downstairs for everyone. Plus the backyard had a pool and a gazebo for anyone who desired a bit of fresh air.

By the time Cicely's crew arrived, there were more than fifty students in attendance. The music was perfectly loud. Everyone was in good spirits. The crowd seemed to implode around them when they saw that Cicely and Toya had hit the scene.

"*Oh my God*! I thought you weren't coming!"

Girls and boys rushed forward to hug and ogle the bad girls. They wanted to know if they got arrested, how they felt about missing graduation, what their parents had to say about the punishment and all things in between.

Cicely and Toya relished being the center of attention. They lived for this. Sandra watched as they struggled to entertain all of the questions, much like pop stars who arrived at the airport to find throngs of their fans waiting.

Sandra felt like she was part of the hubbub at first. But as the crowd pushed forward, she felt herself being relocated to the outskirts, until she was part of the crowd herself, rather than standing beside Toya and Cicely.

That was okay though. Her friends were popular, and she knew that she was part of their clique. She laughed when Toya told them, "Y'all should've known you can't get rid of me that easily!"

Sandra took another sip of her punch, unaware that she too had attracted a little attention. Brandon Carr, a notable screwball, pushed his way through the crowd until they were standing face to face.

"Hey, Sandra!" He had to raise his voice above the music.

"Hi," she told him. Brandon was topless, wearing a pair of swimming trunks and flip flops. He had dark skin that looked rather scrumptious tonight.

"What you drinking?" he asked her.

She smiled naughtily, and he knew.

"Can I taste it?" he asked.

Sandra shrugged and passed him the plastic bottle. It was still half full. She started to tell him what was inside, but she figured he'd find out when he took a sip.

Brandon took a healthy swig of the punch and smiled radiantly. He leaned close to Sandra's ear and told her, "I'll be right back! I need to find a cup."

She nodded. Brandon turned and disappeared in the sea of people. Sandra had a feeling she just got ganked for her drink. She figured that might be for the best. She wasn't sure what it was like to be drunk or buzzed, but she knew that she felt really good. The way Toya and Cicely stole the spotlight usually made her feel awkward. But at the moment, she was cool with it. She couldn't wipe the smile off her face.

Her friends finally broke away from their admirers and found her in the crowd.

"Where's my bottle?" Toya asked.

Sandra shrugged. "I gave some to Brandon, and he took off with it."

"What? Girl, you got *got*?"

"Yeah," Sandra said with a laugh. "I think so."

Toya grinned at her. "You alright? You look faded."

"Really? No, I'm fine."

"Your eyes look glassy," her friend reported.

Sandra shook her head. "I don't feel different."

"You want some more?" Toya asked her.

Sandra nodded. Her friend took her hand and led her through the living room. In the kitchen they found a plethora of goodies; everything from pizza and hot wings to candy and cake. There were a lot of kids in there chowing down. William's mom was there as well. She was a middle-aged woman with long, blonde hair, big boobs that were probably fake and a fresh tan that actually did improve her appearance. She was busy cleaning up after the partygoers. She didn't look like she was hopped-up on her happy pills, but the night was young.

"Hi, Miss Prince," Toya told her.

"Good evening," the lady replied. "And who might you be?"

"I'm Toya. This is Sandra."

"Nice to meet you both! Are you having a nice time?"

"Yes. We just go here. Your house is awesome!"

"Thank you very much."

"We were looking for the drinks," Toya said, and then she noticed a huge punch bowl on the counter. "Is this it over here?"

"Yes," the woman said. "I just made it."

Toya and Sandra grabbed a couple of cups and filled them with what looked like Kool-Aid. They sipped on the way out of the kitchen and noticed the punch had Sprite in it too.

"It's good," Sandra said.

"It's *basic*," Toya said with a frown. "Come on."

She continued to lead the way through the house, which was so packed in some areas they had to squeeze by. Sandra marveled at all of the eyes that were glued to her and Toya. Most of the students had never seen them in bikinis. Apparently they liked what they saw. Jeremy Miller, another perpetual hooligan, looked like he wanted to devour them. Sandra felt like she wanted to let him.

Toya finally stopped walking when she ran into a senior named Corey Craig. He was a brown-skinned pretty boy with a short afro.

Toya stepped to him and asked, "Where it's at?"

Corey's eyes narrowed. "What you talking about?"

She held up her cup. "You know what I'm talking about."

He looked her up and down and smiled. "Come on," he said and led them in the opposite direction.

He stopped at a hallway bathroom and knocked on the door. No one answered. He stepped inside and gestured for the girls to join him. He told Sandra to, "Close the door," and she did so. Corey wore baggy camouflage shorts that had bulging thigh pockets. He produced a small bottle of liquor from each of them.

"What y'all want," he asked, holding the bottles up. "Tequila or vodka?"

"Tequila," Toya said.

Sandra had never tasted tequila, so she stuck with vodka.

The girls offered their cups, but he didn't pour right away.

"You know what I want," Corey said.

Toya shook her head in annoyance, but it was clear she was accustomed to his terms of business. She turned her back and instructed Sandra to, "Turn around, so this pervert can feel your booty."

Sandra was shocked by the request, but in a way she found all of this very thrilling. She turned slowly and kept her eyes locked on Toya's. Corey placed his bottles on the sink for a moment, to free up his hands. Sandra was vaguely aware that this was borderline prostitution behavior when Corey reached with both hands to cop his feel. But there was no sex involved, so she knew it wasn't that bad. She was giggling when she turned back to him to retrieve her liquor.

Corey poured a generous amount in both of their cups and told them, "Come back anytime. I got some more in the car, if I run out."

"Yeah, I bet you'd like that," Toya said as they exited the bathroom.

"Of course I would," Corey readily agreed. "I'd like it a lot!"

CHAPTER SIXTEEN
PARTY OVER HERE!

Somehow I got invited to party
It was exactly what I thought it would be
Kids were popping pills and drinking
A lot of them were smoking weed
Everyone was turnt
I had to join in
I walked in the kitchen
And poured me some gin

Over the next couple of hours, the party swiftly shifted from *happening* to *out of control* to a virtual *madhouse*. More people started to show up, and William gradually lost control over who was allowed to enter his home. It didn't help much that his mother started to zone-out around eleven-thirty.

Sandra watched her for a while, to see if she was popping pills or smoking something. She never witnessed her doing either, but it was clear that Miss Prince was on *something*. She began to float from room to room like a fairy, imploring the students to, *"Get up and dance! Come on, everybody! Let's get it on! Don't sit there like a bump on a log!*" She aggressively went after kids who looked bored. She pulled them off the couch and asked them to, *"Teach me some of your new dances!"*

A crowd of students gathered around and laughed as Kiesha Parks tried to teach Miss Prince the *Nae Nae*. The woman didn't have enough rhythm to pull it off, but she had a lot of fun trying.

Most of the students found her amusing, but it was clear that William was not a fan of his mom's antics. Sandra watched as he waited for an opportune moment to pull her aside and tell her, "Mom, you promised you wouldn't do this."

"What do you want me to do?" she asked, with more volume than was necessary. "Go upstairs and sit there? Is that what you want?"

"Leave her alone!" one of the students shouted.

"Yeah, your mom's cool!" another agreed.

"See, *I'm cool!*" Ms. Prince told her son, much to the amusement of everyone who was watching them.

William shook his head in exasperation and walked away. But it didn't take long before his mother took his advice. By midnight she was nowhere in sight. Some said she passed out in her bedroom. Others tried to start a rumor that she was upstairs with a few horny students. But there were no students unaccounted for, so the gossip didn't gain any traction.

It was around this time that Derrick and his rowdy comrades rang the doorbell and then entered the home when no one answered. William rushed to see who it was. He was none too pleased when he laid eyes on them.

"Hey, uh, what are you guys doing here?"

"We came for the party," Chris told him.

"Ain't this where the party at?" Kevin asked. He tried to step past him, but William stepped to the side and impeded his progress.

"Yes, but I didn't invite you..."

William wasn't sure where he found the courage to stand up to the jocks. At school they used to bully him mercilessly. But this was his home, and he knew he had certain rights here. If worse came to worse, he could ask him mom to kick them out. Or he could call the police, if his mother didn't want to do it.

"Why you tripping?" Derrick asked him. "Ain't this party for seniors? You trying to say we're not your friends?"

William felt fearful and unsure of himself, which were emotions he hated to feel on his home turf. Derrick was tall, dark and menacing. He was smiling, but it was clearly a crocodile smile.

"He, he doesn't go to our school," William said, referring to the fifth person they brought with them. The stranger looked like he might still be in school, but it definitely wasn't at Finley High.

"That's Dante," Chris said. "He's my cousin. He gave us a ride."

"This party's only for students at *our* school," William insisted.

"He gave us a ride," Chris repeated. "If he go, we all gotta go."

William thought that sounded like an excellent idea.

But Derrick told him, "C'mon, man. I know we haven't always been cool with you, but we finna graduate. Can't we let bygones be bygones?"

William checked the time on the grandfather clock in the foyer. "It's already after midnight," he told them. "I was about to shut the party down anyway..."

"Then let us come in and say goodbye to a few people right quick," Rodney suggested.

William cringed inwardly. He didn't think they'd call his bluff. The party wouldn't officially end until two a.m.

"Alright, fine," he grunted. "But don't start any trouble..."

The jocks pretended not to hear that second part as they marched past him and joined the party.

At the same moment, on the other side of the house, Sandra's friend Peter finally mustered up the courage to speak to her. He was already at William's house when she, Toya and Cicely arrived. Each time he tried to approach her, Sandra was busy talking to someone else.

Peter had always been shy, so he waited and watched her from afar. He didn't know Sandra was a drinker, but by midnight she was on her third cup of punch. With William's mom incapacitated, the main punch bowl in the kitchen had been spiked to perfection. You could hardly taste the alcohol, unless you were a newbie who didn't drink at all.

"Hi," Peter said as he took a seat next to her in the den.

This was now the coziest room in the house. Someone had turned the lights off in there, so the only illumination came from the television. There was plenty of seating. Couples were making out in every direction.

"Hey!" Sandra said to her friend. "Where you been? I was looking for you!"

Peter thought Sandra looked beautiful tonight, especially with her bikini top on. But she was unusually loud, and it wasn't hard to figure out why. Sitting so close to her, he could smell the alcohol on her breath.

"I've been here all night," he said. "Have you been drinking?"

"Everybody is," Sandra said with a chuckle. "You want some?"

She offered him her cup. Peter took it, but he set it aside.

"No, I'm good," he told her. "Are you alright?"

She nodded. "Yeah, I'm alright. Don't I look alright?"

He smiled. "Yeah. You look great. Are you getting in the pool?"

"Nope," she said. "I wore this for you."

Peter couldn't hide his elation or his confusion. "For me?"

"Yeah," Sandra said. "You don't like it?"

"You, you mean your swimsuit?"

She nodded. "Yeah."

Peter couldn't believe she wanted him to look at her chest. He didn't consider himself a pervert, but that was an offer he couldn't refuse. Sandra didn't have the biggest breasts at school, but they were a solid B cup. Plus it was a little chilly in the den. Peter felt himself becoming aroused, which was embarrassing. He looked away, blushing.

Sandra reached and touched the side of his face, turning his head back towards her.

"What's wrong?" she asked. "You shy?"

He nodded. "Yeah. I am."

"You don't have to be," she told him. "You can touch me, if you want."

Peter's eyes widened. He didn't know how to respond to such a bold invitation. Sandra giggled. She couldn't believe she said that, either. She knew the alcohol in her system was giving her liquid courage. It felt good to be daring and sure of herself. Peter looked around warily. It took a lot of willpower to keep his hands to himself.

"Where are your friends?" he asked.

"Why? You like Toya?"

"No. I didn't – I like you, Sandra."

She beamed. "I like you, too!"

Peter's chest swelled. He didn't think this would go so easily. But maybe it was *too* easy.

"Come here," Sandra said.

She grabbed his collar roughly and pulled him closer. Before he could react, she planted her lips on his. Peter's eyes were as big as quarters. His mind spun with emotions. He thought their first kiss would make him happy, but this wasn't right. It got even worse when she forced her tongue into his mouth.

He pulled away from her. Sandra frowned and was slow to open her eyes.

She asked, "What's wrong?"

"You're too drunk," Peter told her flatly. "I think you need to go home."

The hurt look in her eyes nearly broke his heart, but he had to stick to his guns. He knew who Sandra was, and this wasn't her. The person he was with now was nothing more than a huge list of regrets waiting to happen. He stood and backed away from the couch.

"I'm going to find your friends. I'll be right back."

Sandra continued to pout like a pound puppy as he turned and left the room.

• • • • • •

Peter didn't find Sandra's friends in the kitchen or at the pool. He was headed to the living room when the first tremors of a commotion began to build. By the time he made it there, there was a horde of excited students rushing to the front door. So far they had all bottlenecked in the foyer. Peter was not surprised to find Cicely and Toya leading the pack. The girls were yelling and cursing profusely. William was trying his best to keep them from going outside.

"What happened?" Peter asked the guy next to him.

"Alma's out there! *They're gonna fight!*"

Peter had more pressing matters on his mind. He didn't want to get caught up in this foolishness, but it was impossible not to watch Toya and Cicely acting wild and deranged – especially since they were the very people he needed to speak to.

In the meantime Chris and his homies were on the prowl. They considered the girl fight a distraction rather than entertainment. Everyone knew Toya was the freak of the week. Derrick had knocked her off several times. He was in the process of grooming her to be more friendly with his friends.

Chris knew Cicely and Toya would get kicked out of the party, if they got into an altercation with Alma. If that happened, he and his crew would follow them, to find out what their after-party plans were.

Or maybe they didn't have to wait until then. As he and Dante strolled through William's home, they spotted a straggler sitting alone in the den. Sandra was sipping a cup of punch through a straw. Chris nudged his cousin with his elbow and nodded at her. Dante was confused. He stopped in the doorway of the den and watched Chris lay the mack down. It didn't take long. Within a couple of minutes the girl was laughing and flirting back.

Chris had a travel-size bottle of tequila in his pocket. The girl accepted it graciously and turned the bottle up until it was empty. Dante heard her ask if he had anymore. Chris didn't, but his cousin did. He looked back and gestured for him to join them on the couch. Dante came and sat on the girl's other side.

Sandra looked over at him wistfully. "Hey. What's your name?" Her smile was big and dopey. Her breath reeked of liquor.

"I'm Dennis," Dante told her. He grinned warmly. "You want some more to drink?"

Sandra nodded. "Yes."

Dante wasn't sure how she managed to slur the one word, but she did. He dug in his pocket and pulled out another travel-size bottle of tequila. He opened it and handed it to her.

"You old enough to drink that?" he asked as she guzzled the liquor like it was water.

"Are you old enough?" she asked him when she was done.

"Yeah," Dante said with a chuckle. "I'm old enough for a lot of stuff."

"Yo," Chris said, feeling neglected. "What about me?"

The room spun when Sandra turned back towards him.

"I didn't forget about you," she managed. "I like you."

She placed a hand on his thigh. Chris looked over her shoulder and raised an eyebrow. Dante gave him a nod, which Chris interpreted perfectly: *She's ready.*

William managed to quell the commotion at the front door fairly quickly, but Peter was still unable to reach Toya and Cicely. After Alma left, they were the center of attention again. Everyone wanted to know what had happened. Toya appeared tipsy as she told the story in great detail.

Frustrated, Peter returned to the den to check on Sandra. His heart sank to the pit of his stomach when he saw her walking out of the room. Her legs weren't steady, but she was in no danger of falling, because she had two escorts. One of them was a boy Peter had never seen before. The other was a jock named Chris, who Peter never got along with.

"Hey, you leaving?" Peter asked her.

"Watch out," Chris said as they walked by him. He had an arm around Sandra's waist, but they weren't moving in sync. They looked like a clumsy three-legged race.

Peter started to follow them, but the guy he didn't know turned and fixed deadly eyes on him.

"Say, move around, punk," he warned.

Peter still might have put his Hero hat on, but Sandra looked back at him and laughed.

She looked him in the eyes and said, *"Peter, Peter, pumpkin eater!"* in a cruel, sing-song voice that struck an uncomfortable chord with him – probably because it was the same way Valerie Mitchell used to make fun of him in middle school. That was another crush that had ended badly for Peter. When they were alone, Valerie said she liked him. But when they got around the popular kids, she hopped on the bandwagon of people who made fun of him. She told them she would *never* go out with such a loser.

Peter's face burned with embarrassment, which easily transitioned into anger. He shook his head as he watched the threesome disappear around the corner. He would've sworn Sandra was different, but he should've known better. Her best friends were the biggest thots at Finley High. Birds of a feather always flocked together.

A part of him wanted to defend Sandra anyway. She clearly wasn't in her right mind. But was she worth taking a punch to the nose for? Hell no. It wasn't his job to save the world or to save a ho.

CHAPTER SEVENTEEN
SWIMMING POOL
FULL OF LIQUOR

I get turnt every day now
It's been like a year
I'm a pro at rolling blunts
And I love drinking beer
I don't have to be at a party
This has become my new life
I'm thinking about dropping out of school
You wanna know why?
Peer Pressure

By Jasmine Walker

The dustup with Alma was a lot less fruitful than Cicely hoped for. Her nemesis finally showed up to the party at 12:30, specifically to fight, according to one of their classmates who rushed into the house and announced her arrival. But when Cicely and Toya tried to accommodate her, they had William to contend with. William was never forceful or authoritative at school, but tonight he was the king of his castle.

He locked the front door and threatened to call the police if Alma and her friends didn't vacate the premises. Cicely and Toya tried to get past him, but William was nearly frantic in his attempts to keep them inside. His mother didn't come downstairs the entire time. It was amazing that he managed to keep the peace all by himself.

By the time Cicely considered the fact that the house must have more than one exit, Alma took heed and fled the scene. Without throwing any blows, Toya and Cicely felt victorious for vanquishing their foe. In the aftermath of the conflict, they were heralded by their peers. With so much drama going on, it was easy to forget about something insignificant, like your best friend, until Cicely realized she hadn't seen Sandra in nearly an hour.

"Hey," she asked Toya, "what happened to Sandra?"

Toya shrugged. "I don't know. She was here a minute ago."

"When?"

"Just now. When we were about to fight."

"No, she wasn't."

"Hell if I know," Toya said with a shrug. "I could've sworn I saw her. Girl, I'm so high, I don't know what's going on over here." Her eyes were low and tinted red.

Cicely was intoxicated too, but she wasn't drunk or high enough to forget about her friend. Or maybe she was. Sandra's whereabouts hadn't been on her mind for quite a while. She rolled her eyes in irritation. "Come on, help me find her."

"Wait," Toya said. "I need to find Derrick first."

"What for?"

Toya gave her a conniving smile. "You know what for."

"You a freak," Cicely said. She left the room and searched for Sandra on her own.

Five minutes later she returned to the living room and found Toya and Derrick getting cozy on the sofa.

"I can't find her," she reported.

"You check out by the pool?" Toya asked. Derrick was sucking on her neck. She didn't bother to open her eyes.

"Yeah," Cicely said. "She wasn't out there."

"Maybe she went upstairs," Toya offered. "Isn't that boy she likes here?"

"Who?" Cicely asked.

"I don't know his name."

"Who, Chris?"

"No, the other one."

"Peter?"

"Yeah," Toya said. "Him."

"Girl, get up!" Cicely said, grabbing her arm.

She pulled Toya to her feet. Derrick did not approve.

"Hey, what's the problem?" he asked.

Cicely ignored him. "Help me find Sandra," she told Toya.

"Why I gotta help?" Toya complained. She took a wobbly step and leaned on her friend for support.

"You're the one who was getting her drunk!" Cicely stated.

"You the one who got her high," Toya pointed out.

"I know," Cicely said. "What if she's passed out somewhere?"

"Then she'd be easy to find," Derrick commented. "It's kinda hard to miss a passed-out chick on the floor."

"Shut the hell up," Cicely told him, and then she realized he might actually be helpful. "Is your friend Chris here?"

"Yeah," Derrick said.

"Where is he?"

He shrugged nonchalantly. "He ain't in my pocket."

"I can't stand you," Cicely snarled. She drug Toya away. "Come on, girl."

Having two sets of eyes wasn't immediately fruitful, but they did get a few promising leads. Someone said they saw Sandra in the den with Peter. But she wasn't there when her friends entered the room. They went out to the pool again, which was where half of the party had migrated to. Sandra wasn't lounging on any of the beach chairs, and thankfully she wasn't lying lifeless at the bottom of the pool.

"This is your fault," Cicely told Toya.

"What? How?"

"'Cause you got her drunk, and you didn't even look after her!"

"I didn't get her drunk. I gave her *one drink*. Maybe two. She got the rest on her own."

"But you knew she was drinking, and you didn't stay with her."

"What about *you*?" Toya spat. "You been trying to get her high all year! I'm not the one who put a blunt in her hand."

Cicely started to say something, but her mouth snapped closed. That was sad but true. They were both irresponsible friends.

"Alright, calm down," Toya suggested. "We know she didn't leave, so she has to be here somewhere."

"How do you know she didn't leave? Someone could've taken her out the back." Cicely's head was spinning. She knew she'd have an easier time with this if she was sober.

"You think somebody kidnapped Sandra?" Toya thought that was farfetched.

"All I know is if something happened to her, it's our fault."

Toya couldn't deny that, so they headed back inside the house, in search of William this time.

They entered the kitchen, and Cicely's eyes widened when she spotted Peter hanging out near the microwave.

"Hey!"

She ran to him so quickly, Peter brought a hand up, expecting a blow.

"What? What I do?"

"Have you seen Sandra?" Cicely asked him.

He frowned, and his mood became somber. "Yeah. She's with Chris and them."

"What? Chris and who?"

"I don't know that other guy. He doesn't go to our school."

"What do you mean she's *with* them?" Cicely asked. She was growing more worried by the second.

"She walked off with them," Peter stated. "I don't know where they went."

"When?" Cicely demanded.

"I don't know. About ten minutes ago. She was drunk."

Cicely's jaw dropped. "*And you let her go with them?*"

"What was I supposed to do?"

"I don't know," Cicely said sarcastically. "Stop them, maybe?"

"She wanted to go," Peter said. But as he thought about it, he knew that might not have been the case. Sandra could barely stand up the last time he saw her.

Cicely shoved him in the chest unexpectedly. She pushed him so hard, Peter took a few stumbling steps back.

"*You wrong!*" she yelled. "You're supposed to be her friend!"

"I, I'm sorry," Peter stammered. "I... I don't know why I didn't do anything."

He felt guilty for not standing up for Sandra when he had a chance. He couldn't tell Cicely that the reason he stood idly by was because he thought Sandra was teasing him. That would make his inaction sound even more cowardly.

"Hey, what's the problem now?" The host of the party stormed into the kitchen looking older than his eighteen years. William's party had been a lot more stressful than he envisioned. Cicely and Toya were the cause of much of his grief.

"Our friend Sandra is missing!" Cicely told him. "He let her go off with Chris, even though he knew she was drunk!"

"It's not my fault!" Peter said.

"What do you mean she's drunk?" William demanded.

"Dammit, she's drunk!" Cicely spat. "Everybody's drunk! This punch bowl is full of liquor. Don't act like you don't know!"

"Alright, chill out," Toya said, stepping between them. "Let's just find Sandra. That's the only thing that matters right now."

Everyone silently agreed that was true. They split up and resumed their search. Back in the living room, Derrick confirmed that Chris' cousin Dante brought them to the party, and he might be the stranger Peter was referring to. They followed Derrick outside and were slightly relieved to find Dante's car still parked on the curb down the street.

In the meantime William went upstairs to check all of the bedrooms and bathrooms. He found his mother sleeping peacefully in the master bedroom. She didn't stir when he opened her door, most likely because she was under the influence of a Xanax problem that was getting increasingly harder to hide. He decided not to wake her. Not now anyway.

On the ground floor, Peter was nearly desperate in his search for a girl who might be worth saving after all. Cicely made him feel like he was completely responsible for Sandra's predicament. Although he knew that wasn't true, he couldn't shake the guilt that was smothering him like a sleeping bag.

Peter, Peter pumpkin eater.

The more he thought about it, the more he realized that sounded like a cry for help rather than an insult. He had heard how badly Sandra's words were slurred. He knew what Chris' intentions were, but he didn't do anything about it. And why? Because he thought Sandra was making fun of him? That was ludicrous. Peter couldn't believe he'd been such a jerk.

His eyes were wild and distressed when he ran into William again in the backyard.

"Did you find her?"

William shook his head. "No. She's not in the house."

"Man, what the hell?"

"I know," William said. "I don't know what else to do."

"What's that?"

William followed his eyes. "That's the pool house. But it's locked. Nobody's in there."

"Did you check?"

William shook his head, and the boys felt the same sense of dread wash over them. They hurried to the small house. But as William indicated, the door was locked.

"See, I told you—"

"Wait!" Peter inched his face closer to the door. "I thought I heard something in there."

William's heart was thundering. He balled his trembling fingers into a fist and knocked on the door.

"Hey, is somebody in there?"

There was no response, but Peter heard another sound come from inside. This time they both heard it.

"*Aww man,*" William muttered. "Let me, I'll go get the key."

As he turned to walk away, the horror and guilt and embarrassment that had been squeezing Peter's heart finally got the best of him. The adrenaline rushing through his bloodstream set his whole body on fire. Without a release, he felt like he would explode.

He turned and pounded on the door with both hands.

"*We know you're in there! Come out!*"

Beyond the sounds of his small fists hammering the door, they now heard murmured voices coming from inside the pool house. Peter doubled-down on his efforts and began to kick the door in addition to knock.

"*Come out of there! Leave her alone!*"

The commotion got the attention of all of the kids around the pool. Cicely and Toya ran outside in time to see Chris open the door of the pool house and emerge with sweat on his brow. He was stunned to see so many people watching him. He looked fretful and hesitant. His cousin Dante was still zipping up his pants when he followed him out. Rather than feel guilty about their predicament, he glared at Peter.

"Man, what's your problem, cuz? She wanted to go!"

With his teeth bared and his eyes filled with fury, Peter did something he had never done to any of the bullies who had targeted him from grade school all the way through high school.

He struck back.

He didn't mean to. His arm seemed to move on its own accord. One second his hands were down by his side. The next second his fist shot up like a rocket and slammed into Dante's chin. The impact sounded like a muffled crack of lightening. The older boy's expression went completely blank.

Peter's chest heaved. He expected to get pummeled by the brooding stranger. But Dante's eyes rolled to the back of his head, and his body dropped lifelessly to the ground, as if someone abruptly cut his puppet strings.

CHAPTER EIGHTEEN
THE FINAL CHAPTER
DETOX

Chris dipped. No one bothered to stop him as he hurried inside the house to retrieve his crew.

Peter was the first to step past Dante's body and enter the pool house.

Inside, it was very dark.

● ● ● ● ● ●

A black and white police cruiser blazed down the highway. It was nearly two a.m. On a weekday, Interstate 35 would've been mostly empty at this time of night. But it was late Friday/early Saturday, and there were plenty of people still on the road. Many of them were leaving some of Overbrook Meadows' happening night spots. Some of the drivers on the freeway that night were drunk, but the police cruiser didn't slow down enough to scrutinize them.

Inside the black and white Dorothy Barnett gripped the steering wheel so hard her fingertips were becoming numb. She wore her full uniform. She still had an hour left in her shift when she got the call. It was the call she always dreaded.

She knew Sandra was alive, and she was grateful for that. But the answers she didn't have threatened to break her down. Tears streamed down her cheeks. Her heart thumped sickly beneath her bulletproof vest. Above her, the lights on her patrol car flashed white and red and blue.

She should've turned the sirens off. Not only was she not currently on duty, but technically there was no emergency. Sandra was at the hospital, and she was safe, and she wouldn't get better any sooner if her mother arrived in thirty seconds or thirty hours. But Dorothy kept her sirens on anyway. She had to.

That was her baby, and her baby needed her.

● ● ● ● ● ●

Sandra was unresponsive when her mother arrived at Jackson Memorial. The doctors said her blood/alcohol level was nearly three times the legal limit. There was no easy fix that would bring her out of her unnatural slumber, which her mother thought looked too much like a coma. All the doctors could do was give Sandra IV fluids to gradually dilute the alcohol in her bloodstream. They checked her blood/alcohol level every hour or so to confirm that the IV fluids were working.

In the meantime they examined her for any signs of sexual assault, which thankfully came back negative. That finding matched statements given by her would-be assailants. During questioning at the police station, one of her classmates named Chris Dorries indicated Sandra wanted to have sex with him, but she passed out before they could commence the act.

Chris denied that he and his cousin Dante planned to take advantage of Sandra in her drunken state. That contradicted witnesses who said Dante was "zipping up his pants" when he emerged from the pool house. But since no assault had taken place, the police didn't have enough evidence to charge either of the young men with a crime.

Sandra's brother Calvin still wanted to "touch up" the boys for plying her with alcohol and taking her to the pool house, but his mother was adamantly against that.

"Her friends said she was drinking and smoking weed before they even got to the party," she told him as they sat at their loved one's bedside.

"Smoking *weed*?" Calvin found that hard to believe.

"I didn't believe it either," Dorothy said. "But they found it in her system." Her dark eyes were wet and unblinking.

Sandra was still unconscious at the time. The doctors were content with letting her come out of the stupor on her own. In the three hours she'd been at the hospital, they'd managed to cut her blood/alcohol level in half. They were confident she would wake up within another couple of hours or so.

"And they tried to, to..."

Calvin was unable to say the "**R**" word. So far everyone they spoke to seemed to avoid it. *"Sexual assault"* was just as bad. But somehow the "**R**" word sounded more sinister and evil.

"But they *didn't*," Dorothy reminded him.

She was the only uniformed officer in the room now. Her colleagues had come to the hospital; first to determine if there was an assault and then to comfort their colleague. But as the wee hours of the night rolled into Saturday morning, Dorothy sent them all away. Sandra didn't need a strong show of force anymore. She only needed to wake up.

"I know you're not okay with what they did to her," Calvin told his mother.

Dorothy shook her head wearily. She had dark bags under her eyes from the lack of sleep and stress the ordeal had caused.

"Those boys aren't getting away with anything," she assured him. "They were taken to the police station and questioned. Their mothers had to pick them up, so their families know what they did – or what they tried to do. You know God works in mysterious ways. If they didn't learn their lesson tonight, rest-assured they'll get what's coming to them. You and I don't have to do a thing. But I think they did learn their lesson. They know how close they came to going to prison."

Calvin watched his mother as she spoke. Dorothy always had so much wisdom. She was a strong woman. She had always been, even before her husband passed away and left her to raise four children on her own.

"What about Sandra?" Calvin asked.

He watched his sister as she slept. She seemed so small and fragile. Her lips were chapped. Her eye sockets were dark and sunken. He was happy that she made it all the way to the end of her senior year before she got into any of the risqué behavior a lot of her peers were involved in. But considering what almost happened to her at the hands of her classmates, there would be no kudos coming her way.

"Sandra doesn't know how lucky she is to be asleep right now," Dorothy said, her jaw tightening. "If she was awake when I first got here, I think I would've been the one who got arrested."

Calvin grinned knowingly. Sandra had been through a lot tonight. He knew things would get worse for her when she woke up. He reached and took hold of his mother's hand.

"Don't go too hard on her."

She looked up at him and squeezed his hand, but her eyes didn't register any sympathy. They were still filled with impending doom.

Nope, Calvin thought to himself. *I definitely wouldn't want to be in my sister's shoes right now. No sirree...*

● ● ● ● ● ●

As predicted, Sandra came out of her death-like sleep five hours after she arrived at the hospital. Initially she was too drowsy and confused to know what was going on. She remembered drinking a little before and during the party, but that was all. She couldn't believe she got drunk enough to pass out and end up at the hospital. She was mortified.

Her mother was at her bedside when she opened her eyes, so Sandra knew she was in big trouble. But she didn't understand why her mom looked so sad, rather than furious. Dorothy decided to wait until they got home before she told her the worst of it.

By then it was seven in the morning. Dorothy hadn't slept all night, and it showed in her gaunt features. She and Sandra sat at the kitchen table, but there was no breakfast being served. There were no Saturday morning cartoons.

Sandra's head was throbbing. It was the worst headache she had ever experienced. It felt like she had a multitude of tumors in her brain, throbbing and pinching her blood vessels. Her stomach felt like she swallowed a putrid watermelon whole. These symptoms worsened by the second as she listened to a disgusting story that didn't sound like it could be real. It certainly didn't sound like something that had happened to her.

But Dorothy's demeanor said it was real, and she had so much information. She knew Chris' full name and his cousin's full name. She knew what time Sandra started drinking and what areas of William's house she had been in. Dorothy told her how Chris was sweating when he exited the pool house and Dante was zipping up his pants.

Sandra became so physically ill, she barely made it to the bathroom before vomit spewed from her mouth like a hose. When she looked up from the porcelain bowl, her mother stood in the bathroom doorway with her hands folded over her stomach.

Sandra didn't think her predicament could get any worse, but she was wrong about that. By ten a.m. people started calling to tell her about the pictures.

EPILOGUE

Gracious and dear, consistently loving
Pillar of wisdom, comforting – nothing
Stands test, nor time, nor pain or fire
As does your love. How I desire
Simply to rise – from this dust, this lowly
Life I live and stand, and slowly
Lift my head and see you smile
Your eyes now gleaming at your child

-KTW

If there was a prize for dumb criminals, Chris Dorries would've been that year's recipient. Rather than take comfort in the fact that he'd narrowly escaped a sexual assault charge and stay on the straight and narrow, he couldn't help but brag about his pool house exploits. He even had proof of his dirty deeds in the form of two explicit photographs he took with his cellphone.

In the first one Sandra was lying unconscious on the floor of the pool house. Someone had pulled her bikini top up, exposing her chest. In the second pic Chris crouched next to the sleeping beauty with his hand on her chest.

He sent the pics to Derrick, who swore he would never share them with anyone else. But who could resist? Derrick sent the pictures to his friend Rodney, who showed them to his little brother Fred. In the two hours it took Fred to spill the beans to their mother, Rodney had already sent the pics to another classmate, who forwarded them to a marginal friend named Toya.

Toya couldn't get through to Sandra's cellphone, so she bit the bullet and called her house phone.

"You should know that Sandra's not going to be on the phone any time soon," Dorothy grumbled. She couldn't believe the girl had the audacity to call the very next day.

"Ma'am, please," Toya whimpered. "It's an emergency."

"What's so damned important?! I know it was you who got my baby high last night!"

"It's, there's some pictures, Ma'am. I'm sorry. They, Chris and them took some pictures..."

Two minutes later Dorothy had the incriminating evidence on her own cellphone. Three hours after that Chris found himself at the police station again. This time the detectives had enough probable cause to handcuff him and send him downtown to the big boy jail.

●●●●●●

Sandra's humiliation was incomparable. She cried for over an hour when her mother showed her the pictures. Each time she thought her sorrow was ebbing, she thought of another friend or teacher or family member who might see the pics, and her tears ran anew.

She wished she could stay in her bed, crying and denying until the last bit of her wretched soul came pouring from her eyes. But Dorothy wouldn't let her. At dinnertime she came and sat on the corner of her daughter's bed with disappointment and fury in her eyes, but there was also compassion.

"You can't stay in bed forever, Sandra. You gotta get up and deal with this."

The girl shook her head. *"Please, Mama,"* she bawled. *"I don't want to."*

"You don't have a choice," Dorothy stated sternly. "When you screw up, you have to stand up and deal with the consequences. That's life."

"Everybody saw those pictures," Sandra cried.

"Yeah, they did," her mother said. "And that's gonna be a hard thing to get past. It's gonna be hard for me to ever trust you again. And it's gonna be hard to look your friends in the eyes. But that's what you gotta to do. You gotta move on, Sandra. Starting right now – with dinner."

"I'm not hungry."

"Then get up and come sit there and watch me eat!" Dorothy barked. She was trying to keep her anger in check, but it was difficult. She knew her daughter had been through a lot. But she couldn't ignore the fact that Sandra put herself in a bad situation. "Wash your face first," she said before leaving the room.

● ● ● ● ● ●

Sandra expected the worst in regards to her redemption and restoration of the trust she lost from her mother, but it wasn't all bad.

There were lectures and long talks. A lot of them. There was discipline. Sandra didn't know when she would see her cellphone again. Going out with Cicely or Toya was not up for discussion, not for a while at least. And Sandra was mortified when her mother told her she had to return to school on Monday, to finish her last week at Finley High.

Sandra thought all of the students would point and stare and laugh behind her back. Some did. But most were supportive. After hearing all of the stories and speaking with people who were at the party, they painted her out to be a victim. A lucky, unfortunate victim. Sandra was also relieved to learn that Chris got kicked out of school and graduation. Any student caught sharing or in possession of the pictures he took would face the same fate.

Derrick, Rodney and Kevin were still there, but they avoided Sandra at all costs. They would turn completely around in the middle of the hallway and head the other way, rather than cross her path. Tardiness be damned. Cicely and Toya weren't there to console her, but Serena was. She ate lunch with Sandra every day. By Thursday, Sandra was nearly back to her old self.

"Are you coming to school tomorrow?" Serena asked over a plate of what she hoped was tuna casserole.

Friday was the last day of school. Technically the seniors were required to come for half a day. But a lot of them considered it a skip-day.

"Yeah," Sandra said. "I forgot to get some people in first period to sign my yearbook. Are you coming?"

Serena nodded. "I don't want to miss the last day of school. And I'm staying for lunch too. You know I can't wait to see what the lunch ladies cook up for us," she joked.

Sandra grinned and looked down at today's questionable meal. Serena smiled too.

"Nice to see you smiling again."

Sandra looked up at her. Her mother told her the same thing this morning.

"You still haven't talked to Cicely or Toya?" Serena asked.

"Cicely's been calling the house," Sandra told her. "My mama told her I can't talk right now."

"What about Peter?" Serena said. "You two haven't spoken?"

Sandra shook her head. She looked around, somewhat fretfully, as if Peter might be near them at the moment.

"He saved you," Serena said. "Like a real life hero."

Sandra agreed that was the case. She nodded slightly.

"I don't know," Serena said with a shrug. "If it was me, I think I'd want to thank him."

"People said I kissed him at the party," Sandra revealed.

Serena raised an eyebrow.

"I don't even remember it," Sandra told her. "I kissed somebody, and I don't remember it."

Serena could imagine how awful that must feel.

"They said he pushed me away and went to find Cicely and them," Sandra continued. "If that was all that happened, I'd be too embarrassed to talk to him. But Peter was the first one to see me in the pool house..." She shook her head. Simply thinking about it was humiliating.

"So you're avoiding him?" Serena asked.

"I think he's avoiding me too," Sandra said. "He hasn't tried to talk to me."

"Don't you think you *need* to talk to him?" Serena wondered. "Maybe it's important for your, I don't know, your healing..."

"I'm not scarred," Sandra said honestly. "I got drunk and *almost* got taken advantage of. But I got rescued before

193

anything real bad happened." She smiled weakly. "Mama says I'm one of the lucky ones. I had a guardian angel looking over me that night."

"Yeah, you did," Serena agreed. "And I'm happy for that. Everyone is."

The girls watched each other quietly for a few moments. They had both been through their share of drama in the past few weeks. The smiles on their faces made it clear that they were survivors now, no longer victims.

"Anyway, what's been up with you?" Sandra asked her. "Can you feel your baby kick yet?"

"No," Serena said with a giggle. "I'm not even four months yet. You know I'm not showing."

"Stand up," Sandra told her. "Raise your shirt up. Let me see your stomach."

"I'm not doing that here!" Serena said, laughing.

"Are you excited about graduation?" Sandra asked.

Serena nodded. "Yeah. I'm excited about college, too – even though I'm not going to a fancy-schmancy one like you."

"Texas Lutheran isn't fancy-schmancy," Sandra argued. "It's a local college."

"It's not a college, it's a *university*," Serena told her. "And it is better than the community college. Are you going to stay on campus?"

"My mama says I can't the first year, but if I do good, she'll let me stay there for the other three years."

"That's good," Serena told her. "You can meet new people. Make new friends."

"Yeah, but I don't want to forget about my old friends," Sandra said. "You and me should always stay friends."

"Already," Serena agreed. "For life."

• • • • • •

Sandra graduated on May 29th. The convention center was packed with friends, family and well-wishers. Her grandparents came, along with her brother and her aunts and a few of her cousins.

When the vice principal started calling the students up to receive their diplomas, she asked that everyone hold their applause until the end. But no one did. Sandra was surprised to hear an enormous racket of hoots and cheers when her name was called. It felt like more than half the crowd got involved.

She knew that a lot of people had heard about the incident at William's infamous party. She thought everyone was cheering to show support for her, because they were glad things didn't go any further than the pictures. She was a victim. But she was also a survivor. A warning to others.

Or maybe that's not why they cheered at all.

Either way, Sandra thought it was freaking awesome!

• • • • • •

Over the summer vacation, she was able to regain most of the trust she'd lost on *that fateful night*. Her mother forgave her, as parents are apt to do, and one by one her freedoms were restored. She was even allowed a visit from Cicely.

By then Sandra was focused on moving on. But her friend hadn't had a chance to formally apologize.

"I'm so sorry for what happened! It's all my fault! I never should've let you—"

"It's okay. Girl, it's all over now," Sandra said with a dismissive wave of her hand.

But Cicely still had dreadful images in her head. She saw them carry her friend's unconscious body from the pool house. She had also seen the pictures of Sandra that were floating around the school.

"Are you sure you forgive me?" she asked.

Sandra was surprised to see that she was near tears. "Of course I forgive you. It wasn't all your fault. I knew better. Calm down, crybaby," she said, trying to lighten the mood.

Cicely chuckled and wiped the moisture from her eyes.

"None of that would've happened if I wasn't drunk that night. We should've been looking out for you."

"You didn't force me to drink or smoke," Sandra reminded her.

"Yeah, but we told you to. I know I'm wrong for that. I feel so stupid. The way they did you... God, Sandra... If I was you, I would hate me right now."

"I don't hate you," Sandra said. "I do think you should stop smoking, though."

"I did," Cicely said right away. "I haven't drank or smoked since that party."

"Really?" Sandra was genuinely surprised.

"My mom knew I was messed up when I got home that night," Cicely told her. "She said I made a fool out of her, after she trusted me enough to let me go to the party. She doesn't treat me the same anymore. She acts like she doesn't want me around. I hate it. I feel like I ruined everything."

She began to cry again. Sandra's eyes watered as well. She reached and pulled her friend into a tight hug.

"Please stop crying," she told her. "You can fix whatever's going on between you and your mom. If I can, I know you can. We gotta move on."

When they separated, Cicely wiped her eyes and nodded.

"Are you ready for college?" Sandra asked her, hoping to change the subject. "You're still going, right?"

"Yeah," Cicely said with a shudder. "But it's going to be different than I expected."

"How?"

"I know I won't be going to any of those wild parties," Cicely stated. "And I don't know how much fun it will be, since I'm not getting high..."

"What? Are you serious?"

"Yeah," Cicely said. "I already noticed how different everything is, you know, without weed. It's like the whole world got a little boring."

Sandra chuckled, which made Cicely crack a smile.

"Once you've been off it for a while, things will start being fun again," Sandra predicted. "But don't start smoking again, just because you're bored."

"I won't," Cicely promised her.

"You know a lot of kids at TCU are probably getting high," Sandra continued. "It might be hard to say no to them, especially since you used to smoke all the time."

"No, I saw what peer-pressure can lead to," Cicely said. "I'm not getting sucked into that."

"So I had to be your Guinea pig?" Sandra noticed.

"Don't say it like that."

"No, it's cool," Sandra said. "I know I learned my lesson. If you did too, that's even better..."

● ● ● ● ● ●

A week later Sandra got a call from her other bestie. Toya was always in such a happy-go-lucky mood, Sandra was surprised to hear that she was morose and contemplative.

"What's wrong with you?" she asked her.

"Pregnant," Toya said simply.

Sandra's eyes widened. She was watching television with her mother, but she stood and left the room. Dorothy watched her with obvious interest.

"By who?" Sandra asked when she made it to her bedroom.

"Derrick," Toya said with a sigh.

Sandra felt a heavy, sinking feeling in her gut, as if she was the one who was suddenly with child. This was her second close friend who'd ended up pregnant. Despite all of the bad things that happened at William's party, Sandra had to consider herself lucky, because none of her problems were permanent.

"What, what are you gonna do?" she asked.

"I don't know. I haven't even told my mom. I'm thinking about getting an abortion," Toya revealed.

Sandra's mouth went completely dry. She didn't know how to respond to that.

"That's wrong, ain't it?" Toya asked, sensing her inner turmoil.

"It... I don't know," Sandra said. "It would, I mean, I don't think I could do it. What did Derrick say about it?"

Toya sighed again. This time Sandra thought her breathing had a *wet* quality. She couldn't believe it, but it sounded like Toya was crying.

"He said it's not his," Toya reported. "He said he don't want a baby, and he don't wanna be with me no more."

Sandra's heart broke right along with her friend's. She didn't think Derrick was the most upstanding guy in the world, but she never thought he was that much of a jerk.

"It's my fault," Toya said. "I knew he wasn't about nothing."

We all did, Sandra thought. "I thought y'all used condoms."

"We did. Most of the time," Toya replied with a sniffle.

Most of the time? Sandra couldn't believe Toya wouldn't protect herself. But since there were nude pictures of her floating around, she didn't think she was in a position to condemn anyone.

"You don't have to have an abortion," she offered. "Serena's keeping her baby. And she's going to college, too..."

"I'm just so *mad*," Toya cried. "I didn't think he would do me like this."

"Yeah, he's wrong. But you don't need him," Sandra said, attempting to comfort her friend.

"I know, but still..."

Sandra shook her head. She was torn between feeling sorry for her and wondering if Toya's fast life finally caught up with her.

"Whatever you decide to do, you know I'm here for you," she said.

"Thanks," Toya replied. Her breath hitched. "I'm, I'll call you back."

When Sandra returned to the front room, her mom noticed her mood had changed.

"Who was that?" Dorothy asked.

"Toya," Sandra said as she returned to her seat. "She said she's pregnant."

Her mom frowned and shook her head. "I know you're not surprised to hear that."

"No," Sandra admitted. "She's mad at the boy because he doesn't want anything to do with her. We knew he wasn't any good."

Dorothy made a *hmph* sound through her nostrils. "I guess now she's talking about having an abortion."

Sandra couldn't hide her surprise. "How'd you know?"

"You think Toya's the first girl who didn't give a damn while they were having sex and then wanted to abort the baby afterwards, like it's no big deal? As much as I hate the republicans for shutting down all of the abortion clinics around here, it's people like Toya who makes what they do sound right."

Sandra gave that some thought. As much as she sympathized with Toya, she couldn't deny that her friend made some pretty bad decisions. She could only hope that Toya's latest predicament would lead to changes in her life.

● ● ● ● ● ●

On Monday, August 17th, Sandra began her collegiate career at Texas Lutheran University. She was super excited, and college life proved to be everything she hoped it would be. The campus wasn't as big as TCU's, but it was huge. It took nearly ten minutes to walk from her algebra class in the Baker Building to her religion class in Armstrong Hall.

She took a full course load. To add to her busy schedule, she also got her first job at the Subway restaurant in the student center. Sandra's schedule was so hectic, she didn't get home until after five on some days. She didn't bother to complain to her mom about how much simpler her life would be if she already had a "home" on campus. Dorothy had made a firm decision, and she wasn't going to change her mind.

Plus Sandra felt she deserved the restriction. She planned to keep her nose to the grind and continue to prove herself worthy of the things she did have, rather than complain about what was missing.

There were so many students on campus, it took nearly three weeks before she spotted a face in the crowd that gave her chills. So far there were eight Finley graduates who chose to further their education at Texas Lutheran. The guy she ran into on Tuesday, September 8th made number nine. Sandra's heart froze when they locked eyes. They were walking towards each other, so she couldn't retreat without making it obvious.

But there was no point in avoiding him, was there? Serena was right; this was one part of Sandra's nearly catastrophic night that she had to confront.

She walked up to Peter and offered him a half smile. "Hi."

He sucked air through his nostrils and cleared his throat before replying, "Hey."

Sandra bit her bottom lip, hoping this wouldn't be too awkward.

"I didn't know you were coming here," Peter said.

"Me neither," Sandra said. "I mean, I didn't know *you* were coming here."

"Do you, um, do you like it?" he asked.

She looked around. "Yeah. I like it."

"I wa–"

"Do you?" Sandra asked. "Oh, I didn't mean to cut you off. What were you going to say?"

"No, it's okay. Do I what?"

"Do you like this–"

"Yeah, I do," he said. "I'm sorry. I didn't let you finish..."

Sandra looked down at her shoes. She looked up at him and then over his shoulder.

"Okay, this is awkward," he said.

Sandra didn't want to agree, but there was no denying it. She met his eyes and shifted her weight from one leg to the other.

"Lets, um, let's keep walking," Peter suggested. "Maybe if we're not staring at each other..."

"Yeah, that's a good idea," Sandra said. She started to continue in the direction she was heading but thought that may be rude. "Which way?"

"It doesn't matter," Peter said. He walked alongside her. "Are you on your way to class?"

She shook her head. "No. I was going to study. You have a class now?"

He shook his head.

It was 10:00 on a warm, sunny day. Sandra wore jeans with sneakers and a tight tee. Peter wore cargo shorts with sandals. Sandra had never seen his legs before. They weren't very muscular or hairy. The couple walked in silence, except for the sound of their feet padding the thirsty grass.

They made it almost all the way to the library before Peter built up the nerve to tell her, "I saw you working at Subway last week."

"Really?" Sandra was surprised by that. She certainly didn't see him. "Why didn't you say anything?"

"I didn't know what to say. I didn't want it to be weird, like it kinda is now."

Sandra chuckled slightly. They made it to the steps of the library and stopped again.

"I guess walking didn't help much," Peter noticed.

Sandra grinned. "Come over here," she said, leading him to a shady area near the library's entrance. When they got there, she sighed and looked him in the eyes. "I've been meaning to thank you, for helping me that night."

"Oh, no," he quickly said. "I didn't do anything. I wanted to apologize to you."

Confused, she asked, "For what?"

"Because I let you go with them," he said. "I saw Chris and his cousin walking with you, and I didn't stop them."

Sandra didn't know that. Hearing it now didn't take away from Peter's heroics. "But you came back for me," she said, trying not to sound like a damsel in distress. "They said you beat on the door, and you knocked that guy out."

He shook his head, grinning. "Honestly, I don't know *who* knocked that guy out. The first thing I asked myself after it happened was *Who did that?* It couldn't have been me."

"Yes, it was you," Sandra said, giggling.

"I know, but I'm not like that," Peter said. "I'm not a fighter. I don't know where it came from."

"It came from inside of you," she said. "I'm glad it did. Thank you very much for saving me."

Peter took a deep breath. "Alright. You're welcome." He looked her in the eyes again, and they smiled. "I'm glad you're okay. I'm glad I could help."

Another few moments of silence passed between them. It wasn't that uncomfortable this time.

"I guess I'll go in here..." Sandra said, moving towards the entrance of the library. "It was good seeing you again. Don't run off the next time you see me."

"I won't," Peter promised. He turned and headed down the stairs. Then he stopped and returned to Sandra before she entered the building.

"Uh, you know, before we went to that party, we talked on the phone a few times, and I was going to ask if you wanted to, you know, go out with me sometimes."

Sandra could tell that he'd been working hard to overcome his shyness. She was surprised and flattered. Peter was well on his way to becoming a man.

"My number hasn't changed," she told him. "You should call."

His eyes lit up. "Really?"

"Of course. Who wouldn't want to go out with their hero?"

He blushed. "Okay. That's cool," he said, trying to downplay the trumpets that were blaring in his heart. "I'll give you a call then." His smile was nearly as bright as the sun.

"Did I really kiss you?" Sandra asked before he could take off. She figured she might as well get that one last bit of awkwardness out of the way.

"Yeah, but I had my eyes open," Peter said, "so it didn't count."

She chuckled. "You had your eyes open?"

"Of course I did. You were acting crazy. You think I'd close my eyes around a crazy lady?"

She laughed. She loved that he could make her do that while discussing something so embarrassing.

"I'll talk to you later," he said and started down the stairs again.

"Don't forget to call me," Sandra called.

"I won't. Sorry, but I'm late for class," he said and picked up the pace.

Sandra's jaw dropped. "I thought you said you didn't have a class right now!" She had to raise her voice because he was jogging now.

"My bad! I lied!" he yelled without looking back.

Sandra shook her head and watched until he was nearly halfway across the big, beautiful lawn. She entered the library with a pleasant smile on her face, a warm feeling in her chest.

Everyone told her college was all about new beginnings. Sandra was happy to see that was true. She suddenly felt optimistic, about school and life in general, like she could be anything she wanted to be. Just like her mom always told her.

KEITH THOMAS WALKER

ABOUT THE AUTHOR

Keith Thomas Walker, known as the Master of Romantic Suspense and Urban Fiction, is the author of nearly two dozen novels, including *Life After, Dripping Chocolate, The Realest Ever* and *Brick House*. Keith's books transcend all genres. He has published romance, urban fiction, mystery/thriller, teen/young adult, Christian, poetry and erotica. Originally from Fort Worth, he is a graduate of Texas Wesleyan University. Keith has won or been nominated for numerous awards in the categories of "Best Male Author," "Best Romance," and "Author of the Year," from several book clubs and organizations. Visit him at www.keithwalkerbooks.com.